Courtside Secrets

Dow Jones

Published by Century Books, 2024.

This is a work of fiction. Similarities to real people, places, or events are entirely coincidental.

COURTSIDE SECRETS

First edition. November 2, 2024.

Copyright © 2024 Dow Jones.

ISBN: 979-8227780843

Written by Dow Jones.

Also by Dow Jones

Breaking the Rules
Courtside Secrets
Love's Dividends

Chapter 1: The Assignment

Alex Mercer sat in his cluttered office, the hum of the city outside barely reaching him over the sound of his own thoughts. As a seasoned sports journalist, he had seen his fair share of stars come and go, but this assignment felt different. The editor had just dropped the news: he was to profile Marcus Greene, the enigmatic superstar of the NBA.

Marcus was a name that floated through every sports conversation, a player whose talent dazzled fans while his personal life remained shrouded in mystery. Known for his incredible skills on the court and a reserved demeanor off it, he was a living legend, yet few truly knew him. As Alex read over the brief, he couldn't help but feel a twinge of excitement mixed with apprehension.

He leaned back in his chair, fingers steepled in thought. What was it about Marcus that made him so elusive? Perhaps it was the pressure of fame, the constant scrutiny that came with being in the public eye. Or maybe there was something deeper—something Alex sensed beneath the surface. He had a reputation for uncovering the human stories behind the stats, but Marcus was different. The player had successfully kept his private life sealed tight, like a vault.

"Think you can crack that vault?" a colleague teased from across the room, breaking his concentration. Alex shot them a wry smile, but inside, he was already formulating questions.

What could he uncover about the man behind the jersey? What was the real story beneath the headlines?

Alex knew that many journalists approached players with a hard-hitting, sensationalist angle, but he preferred to delve deeper. He wanted to find the man behind the legend. But how could he do that when Marcus had so skillfully guarded his privacy?

His phone buzzed, pulling him back to the moment. A message from his editor: "Set up the meeting with Marcus ASAP. Let's make this a piece to remember." Alex's heart raced at the thought. It was one thing to write about Marcus Greene; it was another to sit face-to-face with him.

As he prepared to reach out, a nagging voice in the back of his mind reminded him to tread carefully. This was more than just an interview; it was an invitation to peel back layers of a persona that had captivated the world. But would Marcus allow him in? Would he even want to reveal the man behind the superstar facade?

With a deep breath, Alex composed himself. He couldn't let fear dictate his approach. He would walk into that meeting ready to engage, to listen, and—if the opportunity arose—discover the truths that lay hidden beneath the spotlight.

The thought of meeting Marcus filled him with both excitement and trepidation, but one thing was clear: this was going to be more than just another assignment. It was a chance to uncover a story that could change everything.

The day of the interview arrived, and Alex stood outside the exclusive restaurant where he'd meet Marcus Greene. The sleek glass facade mirrored the bustling streets of the city, but

Alex felt a world apart. Dressed in a tailored blazer, he adjusted his tie, mentally rehearsing his questions. He was determined to break through Marcus's defenses, but he also knew the stakes—this wasn't just another profile; it could be a career-defining moment.

As he stepped inside, the ambiance shifted. The soft chatter and clinking of glasses faded as he scanned the room. There, seated at a corner table, was Marcus. The moment their eyes met, Alex felt a jolt of electricity, an instant recognition that sent his heart racing. Marcus's reputation preceded him: tall, athletic, with an aura of confidence that commanded attention. Today, though, he seemed more reserved, his posture straight and his expression inscrutable.

"Alex Mercer," he introduced himself, extending a hand as he approached the table. Marcus's grip was firm but brief, his gaze unwavering. There was a flicker of curiosity in his deep-set eyes, and Alex sensed a momentary pause, as if Marcus was gauging whether to lower his guard.

"Marcus Greene," he replied, his voice smooth yet cautious. The tension between them was palpable, like an unspoken challenge lingering in the air.

They settled into their seats, the waiter arriving promptly to take drink orders. Alex chose a sparkling water, his nerves making it hard to think of anything stronger. Marcus opted for a glass of red wine, his demeanor calm and composed, yet Alex could detect an underlying tension beneath the surface. This was a man used to scrutiny, and Alex was acutely aware that every word mattered.

"So, Alex," Marcus began, leaning back slightly, his arms crossed over his chest. "What do you want to know about me?"

The question hung in the air, charged with implications. Alex took a breath, determined to steer the conversation beyond the typical surface-level inquiries that athletes often faced. "I'm interested in who you are off the court," he said, meeting Marcus's gaze with sincerity. "What drives you? What keeps you grounded in all this chaos?"

Marcus studied him for a moment, and Alex felt the weight of that scrutiny. He watched as Marcus's expression softened just a fraction, curiosity sparking behind his eyes. "I think everyone sees the highlights," Marcus replied, his voice low and measured. "But they don't see the hard work, the sacrifices. There's a lot more to it than what's shown on TV."

Alex leaned in, intrigued. "What sacrifices have you made?" he probed gently, wanting to elicit more of Marcus's story. He could sense the guardedness in Marcus's posture; he was clearly used to keeping people at bay.

"There's a lot of pressure to maintain an image," Marcus admitted, his gaze shifting to the window for a brief moment, as if he were searching for something beyond the glass. "Sometimes, it feels like there's no room for vulnerability. You have to be perfect all the time."

In that moment, Alex caught a glimpse of the man behind the superstar. It was both exhilarating and heartbreaking. "I can only imagine," he said softly. "It must be exhausting."

Marcus nodded, his expression momentarily vulnerable before the mask slipped back into place. "You learn to cope. You learn to keep certain things private."

The air crackled with an undeniable chemistry, a connection that transcended the confines of their interview. Alex was captivated not just by Marcus's physical presence but by the intensity radiating from him. There was something magnetic about Marcus—the way he spoke, the way he held himself, a mixture of strength and fragility.

As their conversation continued, Alex found himself drawn deeper into Marcus's world. They shared laughs and moments of silence that felt comfortable, even intimate. Yet, despite the rapport building between them, a wall remained, invisible yet palpable.

Time seemed to fly by as they navigated topics ranging from basketball to personal aspirations. Each laugh they shared was like a crack in the armor, and with each passing moment, Alex felt the lines of professionalism begin to blur. But he couldn't shake the awareness of the precariousness of their situation—two men from vastly different worlds caught in a moment of unexpected connection.

As the meal drew to a close, Alex found himself wishing for more time, more opportunities to uncover the layers beneath Marcus's guarded exterior. He knew he was treading on dangerous ground, but he couldn't help but want to explore further.

"Can we meet again?" Alex asked, his heart pounding slightly at the prospect. "There's so much more I'd like to understand about you."

Marcus met his gaze, a flicker of something unspoken passing between them. "I'd like that," he replied, the hint of a smile breaking through the seriousness of the moment.

As they stood to leave, Alex felt a rush of anticipation mixed with uncertainty. He had begun to see the man beneath the legend, but he also sensed that this was just the beginning—a dangerous dance that could lead them both to unexpected places.

As the meal concluded, the waiter cleared their plates, and Alex felt a mixture of satisfaction and regret. He had uncovered glimpses of Marcus's world, yet it felt like they had only scratched the surface. Marcus's demeanor had shifted throughout their conversation—he had grown more open, more engaged—but Alex could still sense the walls around him. It was a delicate balance, and he had no intention of pushing too hard.

"Thank you for taking the time to meet with me," Alex said, a smile breaking across his face. "I appreciate your openness."

Marcus returned the smile, a glint of warmth in his eyes that made Alex's heart skip a beat. "It's not often I get to talk like this. It's refreshing," he replied, his voice low and thoughtful. "You have a way of making it feel... safe."

The word hung between them, charged with meaning. Alex felt a flush creep up his neck, a mix of pleasure and confusion. He had prepared for this interview with the mindset of a professional, yet here he was, feeling something deeper than mere admiration for the athlete. There was a connection, a thread woven through their conversation that both excited and frightened him.

As they stepped outside, the cool evening air washed over them, and Alex took a moment to gather his thoughts. He turned to say goodbye, but something made him pause. He glanced back at Marcus, who was standing just a step away, his expression contemplative.

In that fleeting moment, their eyes locked, and the world around them faded into a blur. There was an intensity in Marcus's gaze that sent a thrill coursing through Alex. It was as if Marcus was silently weighing the possibilities between them, and Alex felt a spark of hope ignite within him. But just as quickly as it ignited, doubt crept in. Was he reading too much into this? Had he crossed a line he wasn't even aware of?

"Uh, I'll reach out to schedule the next meeting," Alex stammered, breaking the spell. He forced a smile, trying to maintain a professional facade while his heart raced. "I look forward to it."

"Me too," Marcus said, his voice softer now, almost intimate. "Take care, Alex."

As Alex turned to leave, he felt a lingering weight in the air, a mixture of possibilities and unspoken words that hung between them. Just as he stepped away, he glanced back and caught Marcus watching him, a hint of something unguarded in his expression—curiosity, desire, maybe even longing. Alex's breath caught in his throat.

What was he doing? This was Marcus Greene, a star player, a man wrapped in fame and expectations. Alex shook his head, trying to dismiss the flutter of excitement that stirred within him. It was foolish to think there could be anything more than a fleeting moment of chemistry. He was a journalist; his job was to observe, not to become entangled in the lives of the people he covered.

Yet as he walked down the street, each step felt heavier with anticipation. His mind replayed the evening over and over, like a highlight reel. Marcus's laughter, the way his eyes sparkled when he talked about his passion for the game, the unguarded glances they shared—it all felt electric. He brushed his hand through his hair, a nervous habit, trying to quell the thoughts swirling in his head.

It wasn't just an assignment anymore; it had turned into something far more personal. The thrill of attraction mixed with the thrill of the story threatened to overwhelm him.

What would happen when they met again? Could he maintain his professionalism while grappling with this unexpected chemistry? Alex shook his head, a smile creeping onto his face despite the uncertainty. He had always thrived on challenges, and this one felt monumental.

As he reached his apartment, he paused at the door, the weight of the night still hanging in the air. He leaned against the wall, letting out a slow breath. No matter how he tried to rationalize it, he couldn't ignore the truth: he was captivated by Marcus Greene, and this was just the beginning.

He couldn't shake the feeling that this was more than just a story. It was the start of something that could change everything. And with that thought, a new kind of excitement filled him—a rush of possibilities waiting to unfold, echoing the heartbeat of the city around him.

Chapter 2: A Second Glance

The days that followed the first meeting felt like a whirlwind for Alex. He could barely focus on anything else, his mind replaying every moment with Marcus Greene—the shared laughter, the glimmers of vulnerability that had pierced through Marcus's otherwise guarded exterior. It was as if a door had cracked open, allowing Alex a glimpse into the life of the man behind the basketball superstar.

Determined to build on their initial connection, Alex wasted no time scheduling follow-up meetings. He sent a carefully crafted email to Marcus, proposing a series of informal interviews that would allow him to dive deeper into both the personal and professional aspects of his life. The excitement that coursed through him as he hit "send" was palpable; he was ready to uncover the story he sensed was waiting beneath the surface.

Within hours, Marcus responded, his message brief but warm. "Sounds good, Alex. I'm game. Let's do this." A smile tugged at Alex's lips as he read the reply. The prospect of spending more time with Marcus sent a thrill through him, blending anticipation with a hint of nervousness.

They settled into a rhythm over the next few weeks, meeting at coffee shops, quiet restaurants, and even a few informal practices where Alex could observe Marcus in his element. Each encounter revealed layers of Marcus that Alex found fascinating. In between discussing game strategies and training regimens, they veered into deeper territory—family, dreams, and the pressures of fame.

During one meeting, while sipping iced lattes on a sun-drenched patio, Marcus opened up about his upbringing. "You know, growing up in the spotlight isn't as glamorous as it seems," he said, his gaze fixed on the bustling street before them. "Everyone sees the success, but they don't see the sacrifices. My family had to make a lot of tough choices for me to get here."

Alex leaned in, genuinely intrigued. "What kind of choices?" he asked, aware that this was a rare moment of honesty. He wanted to encourage Marcus to share, to break down those walls a bit further.

Marcus sighed, running a hand through his hair. "Moving away from home, leaving friends behind... It was all for the game. And now, it feels like I'm always on display. Sometimes I wonder if it was worth it."

The weight of Marcus's words settled heavily in the air between them. Alex felt an urge to reach out, to comfort him in that moment of vulnerability. It was a glimpse of the man behind the public persona—the fears and doubts that lingered despite the accolades.

"Do you ever regret it?" Alex asked, his voice gentle. "The sacrifices?"

Marcus considered the question, his brow furrowing. "Sometimes," he admitted. "But then I look at where I am and the opportunities I have. It's a double-edged sword, you know? It's hard to find a balance."

Alex nodded, the empathy swelling within him. He recognized that beneath the athlete's bravado lay a complex man grappling with expectations. This wasn't just a story about a basketball player; it was about a person who felt the weight of the world on his shoulders.

With each meeting, Alex found himself more drawn to Marcus, captivated not only by his talent but by the depth of his character. There was a warmth in Marcus's smile that lingered long after their conversations ended, and Alex often found himself daydreaming about their next encounter.

As the days turned into weeks, their rapport deepened. They shared personal anecdotes, laughed at inside jokes, and even debated over who made the best coffee in the city. Marcus's guarded nature began to slip away, revealing glimpses of the passionate, humorous man underneath. Each story he shared was a brushstroke painting a more complete picture of his life, and Alex felt honored to be the one to witness it.

But with this growing connection came the realization of how precarious their situation was. Alex constantly reminded himself of the professional boundaries they needed to maintain. He was there to write a story, not to fall into a personal entanglement. Yet every time Marcus's laughter filled the air or their eyes locked in understanding, the lines blurred further, leaving Alex both exhilarated and anxious.

As they wrapped up another meeting one afternoon, Marcus looked at Alex with a sincerity that made his heart race. "Thanks for listening, man. It's nice to talk to someone who gets it," he said, his voice low.

"I'm just glad you're willing to share," Alex replied, feeling a rush of warmth. "I think your story is powerful. It deserves to be told."

Marcus smiled, the vulnerability from earlier giving way to a hint of playfulness. "You just want to get all the juicy details for your article," he teased, but there was no malice in his tone—just a flicker of that chemistry they couldn't ignore.

"Maybe," Alex shot back with a grin, the thrill of their connection igniting in that moment. "But I'm also genuinely interested in who you are."

As they parted ways, Alex felt a swirl of excitement and uncertainty. He was stepping into uncharted territory, where professional boundaries danced perilously close to something more personal. But for now, he was content to explore this path, knowing that with every meeting, they were edging closer to a story that was more than just words on a page—it was becoming a shared journey between two unlikely companions.

As the weeks rolled on, the dynamic between Alex and Marcus shifted from a formal interview setting to something much more relaxed and personal. Their conversations flowed effortlessly, the barriers that had once defined their interactions slowly crumbling. Alex found himself looking forward to their meetings with an eagerness that felt both thrilling and daunting.

One afternoon, as they wrapped up a discussion about Marcus's recent games, Marcus leaned back in his chair, a playful glint in his eyes. "You know," he said, a hint of mischief in his voice, "you seem to have a knack for getting me to talk. I think you've earned a little reward."

Alex raised an eyebrow, curiosity piqued. "A reward? What do you have in mind?"

"How about you join me for a casual outing?" Marcus suggested, a smile spreading across his face. "Just us—no cameras, no fans. A chance to hang out without all the noise. What do you say?"

The invitation sent a rush of excitement coursing through Alex. It was a bold step, blurring the lines between journalist and subject, but he couldn't resist the opportunity to spend more time with Marcus outside of their formal meetings. "I'd love that," he replied, trying to keep his tone casual, though his heart raced at the prospect.

"Great! How about we hit that new arcade downtown? I've heard they have a killer retro game section," Marcus proposed, his enthusiasm infectious.

"Sounds like a blast!" Alex agreed, unable to contain the grin that broke across his face. "I haven't been to an arcade in years."

They arranged to meet later that evening, and as the sun began to set, casting a warm glow over the city, Alex felt a mix of excitement and nerves. This wasn't just an outing; it felt like a step into uncharted territory. He took a moment to compose himself before heading out, mentally preparing for the shift in their relationship.

When Alex arrived at the arcade, he spotted Marcus near the entrance, leaning casually against the wall, looking relaxed in a fitted t-shirt and jeans. The sight of him sent a rush of warmth through Alex, and he couldn't help but notice how effortlessly cool Marcus looked, a sharp contrast to the often-stressed athlete he had encountered in press conferences.

"Hey, you made it!" Marcus greeted, a genuine smile lighting up his face as he approached. There was an ease in his demeanor that made Alex feel instantly at home.

"Wouldn't miss it for the world," Alex replied, feeling the tension from earlier fade away.

They stepped inside, the vibrant sounds of laughter and arcade machines creating an electric atmosphere. Alex felt a thrill of nostalgia as they wandered through the rows of games, each one sparking memories of childhood. Marcus's enthusiasm was infectious, and soon they found themselves engrossed in a competitive game of air hockey, bantering playfully as they took turns scoring points.

"Prepare to lose!" Marcus taunted, his eyes gleaming with mischief as he made a swift shot that sent the puck flying past Alex's defense.

"Not if I can help it!" Alex shot back, his laughter mingling with Marcus's as they played. The game was fierce, but it was clear that neither of them took it too seriously; it was all in good fun.

After several rounds, they took a break, catching their breath and leaning against the edge of a nearby game. "Okay, I'll admit it—you're better than I expected," Alex conceded, wiping sweat from his brow.

"Just wait until I teach you some of my winning strategies," Marcus replied with a smirk, and in that moment, the tension that had previously existed in their interviews felt like a distant memory.

As they moved through the arcade, they shared stories about their favorite games and interests beyond basketball. Marcus revealed his love for classic films, while Alex talked about his passion for writing and how he'd once dreamed of becoming a screenwriter. The more they shared, the more they found common ground, discovering unexpected similarities that deepened their connection.

Eventually, they settled into a cozy booth in the back of the arcade, where they could hear each other over the noise. Marcus sipped on a soda while Alex nibbled on popcorn, and as they chatted, Alex felt the walls that had once defined their relationship fading into the background.

"I always thought athletes were just about the sport, you know?" Alex said, glancing at Marcus. "But you're different. You have so many interests outside of basketball."

Marcus chuckled, a lightness in his demeanor. "Yeah, people forget that we're just regular people too. I mean, I love what I do, but there's more to life than just basketball. I want to explore all the things that make me... me."

Alex nodded, captivated by Marcus's openness. "I get that. It's easy to get pigeonholed in our roles, but it's those little passions that keep us grounded."

As their conversation deepened, Alex felt a swell of admiration for Marcus. This was a side of him that the public rarely saw—vulnerable, genuine, and relatable. It was intoxicating, and Alex couldn't help but feel a growing attraction. The way Marcus spoke, the passion in his voice—it all drew Alex in further, making it harder to maintain his professional distance.

With each passing moment, the boundaries between journalist and subject faded more, and Alex found himself lost in the connection they were building. As they continued to laugh and share stories, he realized this outing was more than just a casual meet-up; it was a glimpse into the possibility of something deeper—a friendship, or maybe more—just waiting to unfold.

And as they finished their snacks and moved back into the thrumming energy of the arcade, Alex couldn't shake the feeling that this evening was a turning point, one that could change everything he thought he knew about Marcus—and about himself.

As the night wore on, Alex and Marcus continued to lose themselves in the arcade's vibrant atmosphere. They played games, cheered each other on, and shared more laughs than Alex could remember having in a long time. The walls that had once separated them as journalist and subject had crumbled to dust, replaced by an undeniable connection that hung in the air like static electricity.

After a particularly competitive round of racing games, they found themselves back at the cozy booth, breathless and exhilarated. Alex leaned back, a wide grin on his face. "I can't believe you beat me again! I thought I had you on that last turn."

Marcus chuckled, his laughter ringing like music in Alex's ears. "You have to learn to take the corners better," he teased, a playful sparkle in his eyes.

Their banter faded into a comfortable silence as they both settled into their seats. The playful atmosphere shifted, and Alex felt a subtle change in the air, as if the arcade around them had blurred into the background. He looked over at Marcus, who was wiping sweat from his brow, his expression softening, revealing a more serious side.

In that moment, the chemistry between them crackled like a live wire. Alex's heart raced as he caught Marcus's gaze, an intensity simmering beneath the surface. He could feel the heat radiating between them, an electric tension that pulsed with every heartbeat. It was as if the world had narrowed to just the two of them, and every fiber of Alex's being screamed to close the distance.

"Alex..." Marcus started, his voice low, but the words hung in the air, unspoken yet laden with meaning.

Before Alex could respond, he sensed the shift—an awareness of the precariousness of their situation. They were teetering on the edge of something profound, something that could irrevocably alter the nature of their relationship. The thrill of the moment battled with the caution of his profession, and suddenly, Alex felt exposed, vulnerable in a way that made him hesitate.

He swallowed hard, breaking eye contact as he focused on the flashing lights of the arcade machines around them. "Maybe we should get going," he said, his voice steadier than he felt. The urge to draw closer, to explore the heat that crackled between them, was almost overwhelming, but the journalist in him knew they were skirting a dangerous line.

"Yeah, you're right," Marcus replied, a hint of disappointment clouding his features, but he quickly masked it with a casual smile. "It's getting late."

They gathered their things, the playful energy from earlier replaced by an unspoken tension that clung to them like a fog. As they walked toward the exit, Alex could feel the weight of the moment hanging heavily between them. He stole a glance at Marcus, whose expression was a mixture of longing and restraint. The air felt charged, and every step brought them closer to the inevitable goodbye.

Outside, the cool night air was a sharp contrast to the warmth that lingered in the arcade. Alex turned to Marcus, their eyes locking once more. The world around them faded away, leaving only the two of them in that moment.

"Thanks for tonight," Alex said, his voice barely above a whisper. "I had a lot of fun."

"Me too," Marcus replied, the sincerity in his tone making Alex's heart flutter. "It's nice to just be... us, you know?"

"Yeah, I get that," Alex replied, his pulse racing. The intimacy of their shared moment felt profound, and he desperately wanted to lean in, to test the waters of their undeniable attraction. But fear of crossing a line held him back, anchoring him in place.

The silence stretched between them, heavy and charged with possibilities. Alex could see the way Marcus's gaze flickered down to his lips, and his breath caught in his throat. It was a moment where everything felt possible—where a single step could change everything.

But as quickly as it ignited, the moment slipped away. With a swift intake of breath, Alex took a small step back, creating distance between them. "I should get going," he said, the words tasting bittersweet on his tongue.

"Right. Same here," Marcus replied, though his voice lacked the enthusiasm it had carried earlier. The weight of unspoken feelings loomed large, and the realization that they were both holding back was palpable.

"Let's do this again sometime," Alex suggested, trying to keep the mood light, even as a part of him ached with the possibility of what could have been.

"I'd like that," Marcus replied, though the light in his eyes dimmed slightly. They stood there for a moment longer, caught in the magnetic pull between them, neither willing to take that final step forward nor retreat completely.

Finally, they shared a hesitant smile, and with that, they parted ways. Alex watched Marcus walk away, the figure of the NBA star fading into the night. A part of him wanted to call out, to bridge the gap that had just formed, but he stayed silent, feeling the weight of the moment settle in his chest.

As he made his way home, Alex couldn't shake the tension that lingered in the air. What had begun as an assignment had morphed into something more complex, a web of emotions and attraction that tangled around them both. He knew this was only the beginning, that the lines they had blurred would only continue to complicate their lives.

And as he lay in bed that night, Alex realized that he was in deeper than he had anticipated, caught between his professional duties and a burgeoning desire that threatened to unravel everything. The question lingered in his mind—could he navigate the treacherous waters ahead, or would their connection lead to an entanglement neither of them could escape?

Chapter 3: First Steps Into Danger

The days that followed the arcade outing were a whirlwind of conflicting emotions for Alex. As he sat at his desk, fingers hovering over the keyboard, he wrestled with the fine line between professional integrity and personal connection. The article on Marcus Greene had taken on a life of its own, evolving into a narrative that was becoming increasingly difficult to separate from his own feelings.

He had started drafting the piece with the intention of presenting a straightforward profile of the NBA star—his career highlights, challenges, and the public persona that captivated millions. Yet, as he sat in his small office surrounded by stacks of notes and research, Alex found himself slipping in subtle hints of Marcus's private life, his vulnerabilities and complexities. It felt wrong, yet it felt so right.

"Marcus Greene isn't just a star athlete," he typed, pausing to consider his words. "Behind the accolades lies a man grappling with the weight of expectation and a yearning for something more." As he wrote, he couldn't help but think of their conversations, the way Marcus had shared fragments of his life, allowing Alex to see the insecurities that often lay hidden beneath the surface.

But with each stroke of the keyboard, Alex felt a pang of guilt. Was it ethical to inject his personal feelings into the narrative? He knew he was skirting the edges of journalistic objectivity, but the more he learned about Marcus, the harder it became to maintain that distance.

He pushed back against the swell of emotion, reminding himself that he was a journalist first and foremost. Yet, as he continued to draft the article, he found his resolve weakening. The connection they had forged in their casual outings had transformed his perspective, making it challenging to approach Marcus as just another subject. Each time he reached for the keyboard, he could feel the warmth of their laughter echoing in his mind, the weight of unspoken words heavy in the air.

Alex glanced at the clock and sighed. He was supposed to meet with his editor later that day to discuss the article's progress, but he felt unprepared. How could he explain the direction the piece had taken? He couldn't admit the emotional stakes he had unwittingly become entangled in, not when the story was supposed to be about Marcus, not about himself.

With a deep breath, Alex refocused, determined to maintain some semblance of professionalism. He had to keep the narrative grounded in facts, in Marcus's accomplishments and challenges, even if his heart begged him to explore the deeper connection that had begun to blossom between them. He continued typing, detailing Marcus's rise in the NBA, his struggles with injuries, and the relentless pressures of fame. Yet, no matter how he tried to steer clear of the personal, the words kept drifting back to the man he had come to admire.

"Marcus possesses an intensity that captivates those around him," he typed, but the sentence felt hollow without acknowledging the man behind the intensity—the vulnerable side that had drawn Alex in. The tension between what he wanted to write and what he felt was becoming increasingly palpable.

As he scrolled through his notes, a voice in the back of his mind reminded him of the consequences of crossing professional boundaries. Alex had seen too many stories tarnished by personal entanglements, too many careers damaged by the blurred lines of objectivity. He could not afford to let his emotions dictate the story he was telling. But the truth was, every time he thought of Marcus, his heart raced, and his thoughts strayed into dangerous territory.

Despite his attempts to stay focused, thoughts of Marcus intruded relentlessly. He couldn't ignore the way their conversations had turned into something more meaningful than a simple interview. There was a warmth in Marcus's gaze that lingered with Alex long after their meetings, a sense of intimacy that left him yearning for more. It was exhilarating and terrifying all at once.

As the afternoon wore on, Alex made a decision. He would include a few more hints of Marcus's personal side in the draft but would couch it in a way that highlighted his resilience and determination. It would be a way to acknowledge the complexity of Marcus as a person while still maintaining a level of professionalism.

When the time came to meet with his editor, Alex felt a knot of anxiety in his stomach. He walked into the conference room, where his editor, Sarah, was already waiting, her expression a mix of curiosity and impatience.

"So, how's the article coming along?" she asked, leaning back in her chair.

"It's going well," Alex replied, his voice steady despite the nerves fluttering inside him. "I've been digging deeper into Marcus's background, and I think I'm starting to uncover some interesting angles."

"Interesting angles?" Sarah echoed, raising an eyebrow. "What do you mean? Give me the highlights."

Alex hesitated, recalling the moments he had shared with Marcus—how the man behind the athlete had begun to reveal himself. But he couldn't say that. "Well, I think it's important to show how he's navigated the pressures of being in the spotlight, especially with his recent injuries and the media scrutiny."

"Good. We need that depth," Sarah said, nodding. "But remember, this is a profile, not a memoir. Stay objective."

"Of course," Alex replied, though he felt the weight of his own words. The pressure to remain objective pressed down on him, but he couldn't shake the feeling that his connection with Marcus was giving him a unique perspective—one that could enhance the story rather than detract from it.

After discussing the article's direction for a while longer, Alex left the meeting feeling a mix of relief and anxiety. He knew he was treading dangerous waters, and yet, he couldn't help but feel that the personal connection he had with Marcus might just be the key to unlocking the story's true potential.

As he walked back to his office, Alex couldn't ignore the rush of emotions that surged within him. He was stepping into uncharted territory, where the lines of professionalism were beginning to blur, and he couldn't help but wonder what lay ahead. With every word he wrote, he was venturing further into the unknown, drawn toward a path that promised both peril and passion—a dangerous game that was only just beginning.

As the sun dipped below the horizon, casting a warm glow across the city, Alex found himself once again stepping into the familiar yet thrilling world of Marcus Greene. Their meetings had become a highlight of his weeks, the anticipation of each encounter pulsing with an energy that made his heart race.

This time, they met at a trendy café near the arena where Marcus played. The atmosphere was lively, buzzing with fans and chatter, but Alex felt an undercurrent of excitement and tension that set his nerves on edge. As he scanned the room, he spotted Marcus at a corner table, his striking features softened by the gentle light filtering through the window.

"Hey, you made it!" Marcus greeted, his smile brightening Alex's mood instantly.

"Wouldn't miss it," Alex replied, sliding into the seat across from him. They exchanged pleasantries, but the air between them crackled with unspoken feelings, a magnetic pull that neither could ignore.

As they talked about everything from basketball to their favorite movies, Alex noticed the way Marcus's gaze lingered on him, the intensity in his eyes sending shivers down Alex's spine. It was as if Marcus was weighing his next words carefully, and Alex felt the tension building with every passing moment.

Finally, after a particularly spirited discussion about a recent game, Marcus leaned in closer, lowering his voice to a conspiratorial whisper. "You know, I've been thinking," he said, his eyes locking onto Alex's. "Why don't we continue this conversation somewhere a bit more private? My suite is just around the corner."

Alex's breath caught in his throat at the invitation. There was an electric thrill at the thought of being alone with Marcus, but a flicker of hesitation crossed his mind. "Is that really a good idea?" he asked, trying to mask the excitement in his voice with caution.

"Why not? It's just us, and I could really use a friend who gets it," Marcus replied, his expression earnest. There was a vulnerability in his tone that made Alex's heart swell. The idea of stepping into Marcus's world, even briefly, felt too alluring to resist.

With a nervous nod, Alex agreed, and they quickly finished their drinks before making their way to Marcus's suite. The walk felt charged, each step echoing the anticipation building inside him. As they reached the door, Marcus paused for a moment, turning to face Alex.

"Are you sure about this?" he asked, his voice low, a hint of concern flashing across his features.

"I am," Alex replied, the conviction in his tone surprising even himself. "Let's do it."

The moment Marcus opened the door, a wave of warmth enveloped them, and Alex stepped into the private world of the NBA star. The suite was tastefully decorated, a blend of luxury and comfort, but all he could focus on was Marcus. The door clicked shut behind them, sealing them into a bubble where the outside world faded away.

As they moved deeper into the suite, Alex felt a rush of adrenaline coursing through him. The air was thick with unspoken possibilities, and he could sense the shift in Marcus as well. It was as if they were both teetering on the edge of a precipice, ready to leap into the unknown.

Marcus stepped closer, his expression shifting from uncertainty to determination. "I've wanted to do this for a while," he admitted, his voice barely above a whisper.

Before Alex could respond, Marcus closed the distance between them, capturing Alex's lips in a fervent kiss. The sensation was electric, igniting every nerve ending in Alex's body. He melted into the kiss, hands finding their way to Marcus's shoulders, anchoring himself in the moment. It was everything he had imagined and more—the heat of Marcus's body, the taste of him, the way their lips moved together as if they were always meant to be.

But as quickly as the kiss ignited, reality crashed back in. Alex pulled away, breathless and wide-eyed, the gravity of what they were doing dawning on him. "Marcus, we can't... What if someone sees us?" he stammered, the thrill of the kiss overshadowed by a rush of anxiety.

Marcus's brow furrowed, a mix of desire and apprehension crossing his face. "I know. I just... I couldn't help it. There's something about you that drives me crazy," he confessed, running a hand through his hair, frustration evident in his posture.

Alex stepped back, trying to regain his composure. "This changes everything. We're crossing a line here, and you know the risks involved. If anyone finds out..."

"I get it," Marcus interrupted, his voice firm but tinged with regret. "But I can't pretend I don't feel this connection between us. We're both adults—we can handle it."

"Handle it? You're an NBA star! Your whole career is at stake," Alex countered, feeling the weight of their situation pressing down on him. The stakes were high, and every instinct screamed that they were playing with fire.

Marcus sighed, the tension evident in his shoulders. "I'm not asking you to throw caution to the wind. Just... can we keep this between us for now? I want to explore this with you, but I don't want to jeopardize your career either."

Alex felt a rush of conflicting emotions—excitement mingled with fear. "I want this too, Marcus, but I need to be careful. This could ruin everything," he replied, his voice softer now, acknowledging the uncharted territory they were entering.

"Then let's keep it our secret for now," Marcus said, stepping closer again, his gaze unwavering. "We can take it slow, see where it goes, but I can't ignore what I feel."

Alex searched Marcus's eyes, seeing the sincerity reflected back at him. It was a dangerous game they were about to play, but the chemistry was undeniable. With a deep breath, he nodded, feeling the rush of adrenaline mixed with anticipation.

"Okay. Our secret," he agreed, the weight of the decision settling around them. "But we need to be careful. No public displays, no hints—at least for now."

"Deal," Marcus replied, a spark of relief in his eyes.

As they stood there, a palpable tension still hung in the air, the thrill of their connection humming between them. With a tentative smile, Marcus reached out and intertwined his fingers with Alex's, the simple gesture sending a thrill through him.

"Let's take this one step at a time," Marcus said softly, and in that moment, Alex knew they were stepping into a world that held both danger and possibility—a world where they would have to navigate their feelings while keeping their budding romance under wraps.

With that silent agreement, they leaned in for another kiss, the heat of the moment enveloping them once more. It was a kiss filled with promise and uncertainty, a beginning that could lead them down a path fraught with complications, but for now, it was enough. They were two souls dancing on the edge of danger, ready to explore the depths of their connection, knowing that the journey ahead would challenge everything they thought they knew.

As the evening wore on, Alex felt the intoxicating mix of exhilaration and trepidation settle in the pit of his stomach. Every kiss they shared seemed to draw him deeper into uncharted territory, and the warmth of Marcus's presence lingered long after their last embrace. However, as Alex reluctantly pulled himself away from the moment, he could already feel the weight of reality crashing back down around him.

"Okay, I should go," he said, trying to keep his tone light, though his heart raced with uncertainty. "We've pushed our luck enough for one night."

Marcus's eyes softened, but he nodded in agreement. "Yeah, I think that's smart." There was a hint of disappointment in his voice that tugged at Alex's heart. "But I'm glad we talked about this. I want to make sure we're on the same page."

"Me too," Alex replied, stepping back toward the door, each movement laden with the knowledge of what they had just crossed—a threshold into a secret that felt exhilarating yet terrifying.

As he left the suite, the cool evening air hit him like a splash of cold water, shocking him back to reality. The streets were bustling with nightlife, a stark contrast to the quiet intimacy he had just shared with Marcus. He took a deep breath, attempting to steady his racing heart, but the exhilaration was quickly overshadowed by a nagging sense of anxiety.

Reaching for his phone to check the time, Alex noticed a new message notification from one of his colleagues at the paper. He swiped to unlock the screen, only to find his stomach drop at the contents of the text:

"Hey, did you hear? The editor's looking into Marcus's love life. Something about a potential article. Be careful!"

The words hit him like a punch to the gut, and his heart began to race even faster. The reality of their secret relationship crashed over him with a ferocity that left him breathless. What if the editor uncovered something? What if their innocent interactions became fodder for a sensational story? The thought of being exposed sent a chill down his spine.

Alex leaned against the side of the building, his mind racing. He knew he had to tread carefully. There was too much at stake—not just for Marcus's career, but for his own as well. The very idea of a public scandal sent a wave of nausea through him.

He quickly typed a reply, his fingers trembling as he struggled to find the right words. *"I'll be careful. Thanks for the heads up."* He hit send and took a moment to breathe deeply, trying to dispel the rush of panic that had set in.

What would he do if the paper went digging into Marcus's life? Would they connect the dots between his article and their clandestine relationship? He felt a surge of protective instinct for Marcus—he didn't want to see him hurt or his reputation tarnished by something that had started as innocent curiosity and quickly spiraled into something far more complicated.

As he made his way home, Alex's mind was a whirlwind of thoughts. The secret they had just agreed to keep felt heavier now, laden with the risk of discovery. He replayed their time together, every shared smile and lingering touch, and while he cherished those moments, he couldn't shake the anxiety of what lay ahead.

His phone buzzed again. This time it was a text from Marcus.

"Hey, just wanted to say I had an amazing time tonight. Let's keep in touch about everything. I don't want to rush anything."

A small smile tugged at the corners of Alex's mouth despite the tension gnawing at him. He quickly replied, *"Me too. Just got a bit of news that has me on edge, but we'll figure it out."*

He pressed send, his heart racing as he contemplated the future. Their connection was undeniable, but the stakes were rising with each passing moment. He was falling for Marcus, and the thought of what could happen if they got caught was both thrilling and terrifying.

As he entered his apartment, Alex knew he needed to be vigilant. He had to navigate the storm brewing around them with caution. The exhilaration of their budding romance was a double-edged sword, and he was all too aware that their first steps into danger could lead to heartache if they weren't careful.

With each text exchanged, each moment shared, the tension hung thick in the air, a reminder of the risks they had taken. They were standing on a precipice, and one misstep could send them tumbling into chaos. Alex resolved to protect their secret, no matter the cost, even as he felt his heart yearning for something more—something real with the man who had unexpectedly captured it.

Chapter 4: Hiding in Plain Sight

In the weeks that followed, Alex and Marcus navigated the delicate balance of their relationship, constantly aware of the eyes that could be watching them. Every interaction had to be meticulously planned, each moment together stolen like precious jewels hidden from the prying eyes of the world. The thrill of their secret kept the spark alive, but it also ignited a sense of urgency and anxiety that threaded through their days.

Alex learned to embrace creativity in their encounters, employing a blend of spontaneity and caution. Their first discreet meeting took place in a small hotel not far from the arena—a place where they could share a few hours of privacy without the risk of being recognized.

The room was dimly lit, adorned with neutral decor that felt both generic and comforting. As soon as Marcus stepped inside, the tension from the outside world fell away. The thrill of secrecy enveloped them, and they quickly fell into each other's arms, sharing heated kisses that melted away the stress of their hidden lives.

"Do you think anyone saw us come in?" Alex asked breathlessly as they pulled apart, their foreheads resting against each other.

Marcus chuckled softly, his breath warm against Alex's skin. "I doubt it. This place is pretty low-key. Besides, we're just two guys hanging out. Nothing suspicious about that."

Alex smiled, reassured by Marcus's confidence. Still, the weight of their secret lingered in the air, a reminder of the stakes involved. They spent the evening wrapped up in each other's warmth, talking and laughing, the outside world forgotten, if only for a little while.

As their meetings progressed, they developed a rhythm that felt both thrilling and risky. Late-night phone calls became their lifeline, moments where they could share thoughts, fears, and desires without the risk of being seen together. The sound of Marcus's voice on the other end sent a rush of comfort through Alex, filling the gaps between their secret encounters.

"Just hearing you makes my day better," Alex would often say, his voice low and intimate, as if they were the only two people in the world.

"Same here," Marcus would reply, the warmth in his tone making Alex's heart flutter. "It's crazy how much I look forward to our calls. It feels like the only time I can truly be myself."

On the sidelines of NBA events, they discovered clever ways to maintain their connection. Alex would often find himself at the games, armed with his notepad and camera, pretending to focus on his work while stealing glances at Marcus. During halftime, they would text back and forth, exchanging flirty banter and stolen moments of longing. It was a thrilling game of hide-and-seek played out in plain sight, and the thrill of it all made Alex feel alive.

One evening, after a particularly tense game that saw Marcus on the court battling fierce opponents, Alex spotted him across the sidelines. Their eyes locked, and for a brief moment, it felt like the world around them faded away. Marcus flashed a quick smile, and Alex couldn't help but grin back, his heart swelling with affection and pride.

"Can you meet me at the usual spot?" Alex texted as he watched Marcus head toward the locker room.

"On my way. Just give me a few," Marcus replied, and Alex's excitement surged.

They had found a small alcove in the arena that provided just enough privacy for their brief meetings. It was a place filled with shadows and secrecy, perfect for their stolen moments. When Marcus arrived, his expression was a mix of exhaustion and exhilaration from the game.

"Hey, you," he said softly, pulling Alex into an embrace that felt like a refuge from the chaos of their lives.

"Great game tonight," Alex murmured, relishing the warmth of Marcus's body against his.

"Thanks. It was tough out there, but knowing I'd get to see you afterward kept me going," Marcus replied, a hint of mischief in his eyes.

As they exchanged whispered confessions and teasing remarks, the outside world faded even more. But with each encounter, the fear of being discovered loomed larger. They both understood the risks involved, but the thrill of their clandestine romance only heightened their desire for one another.

Their secret rendezvous continued, filled with passionate kisses and whispered dreams. They learned to navigate their hidden world, savoring each moment while grappling with the reality that their relationship was built on a fragile foundation.

Yet as the days turned into weeks, Alex found himself struggling with the weight of their secrecy. The exhilaration of hiding in plain sight was intoxicating, but he couldn't shake the feeling that they were always just one misstep away from being caught. The thrill of their love was intertwined with an undercurrent of anxiety, and he wondered how long they could sustain this delicate dance before the pressure became too great.

With each passing day, Alex's feelings for Marcus deepened, and he couldn't help but wonder what the future held for them. The world outside was full of challenges, but in those stolen moments, all that mattered was the connection they shared—a bond that felt both exhilarating and terrifying, a love hidden in the shadows waiting for its chance to shine in the light.

Despite their best efforts to maintain secrecy, the reality of their hidden relationship began to rear its head in unexpected ways. As the weeks went by, Marcus's life off the court became increasingly difficult to manage. The adrenaline of their clandestine meetings was overshadowed by mounting pressure from the outside world, particularly from his agent, Riley.

Riley had always been fiercely protective of Marcus's public image, and as a seasoned professional in the industry, she had an instinct for when things were amiss. It started with subtle observations—Marcus seemed more distracted during practice, his focus wavering at times when it should have been laser-sharp. Then came the questions.

"Marcus, I've noticed you've been disappearing a lot lately," she said one afternoon as they sat in her office, reviewing game footage. "Is there something going on that I should know about? You're acting different."

Marcus shrugged, feigning nonchalance. "Just been focused on my game, you know? Trying to keep my head in the right space."

"Right. But your sudden need for privacy raises flags. We're in a league where the media is always watching. I can't have you off gallivanting—people will start talking," Riley replied, her tone firm but concerned.

He felt a pang of guilt. Every moment spent with Alex had been a breath of fresh air, a temporary escape from the pressures of fame, but it was becoming increasingly clear that maintaining this facade was starting to take its toll.

"I'm not 'gallivanting,' Riley. I just need some space sometimes. Can't a guy have a private life?" Marcus shot back, a hint of defensiveness creeping into his voice.

Riley's gaze softened slightly, but her determination remained unwavering. "I understand that, but if something is happening, I need to know. We have a brand to protect, and if rumors start, it could affect everything we've built."

The conversation gnawed at him as he left her office, a heaviness settling in his chest. Marcus couldn't deny that Riley had a point; he had been more elusive lately, prioritizing his time with Alex over the relentless demands of his career. It was exhilarating and terrifying all at once, but he couldn't ignore the reality that loomed just beyond their bubble.

Later that evening, as he prepared for their next secret rendezvous, Marcus felt a mix of anticipation and anxiety. He arrived at their usual alcove, heart pounding with excitement, but as Alex greeted him with a warm smile, Marcus struggled to fully engage.

"Hey, you okay?" Alex asked, his brow furrowing with concern as he noticed the tension in Marcus's posture.

"Just... work stuff," Marcus replied, forcing a smile as he pulled Alex into a tight embrace, wanting to drown out the noise of his worries. The warmth of Alex's body against his momentarily eased the pressure, but the relief was fleeting.

"Work stuff? You know you can talk to me, right?" Alex said gently, pulling back to meet Marcus's gaze.

"Yeah, it's just my agent, Riley. She's starting to notice my absences. It's becoming harder to keep this hidden," Marcus confessed, the weight of his admission pressing down on him. "She's demanding explanations, and I don't want to give her any."

Alex's expression shifted, concern mingling with frustration. "Marcus, you know this is risky. The more time we spend together, the harder it'll be to maintain our secret."

"I know, but I don't want to end this," he said, his voice firm. "Not yet. Not when things are just starting to feel real between us."

Alex sighed, the tension in the air palpable. "I want this too, but if Riley's catching on, we need to be careful. She's not just your agent; she's your lifeline in this industry."

"I'll talk to her. I can smooth things over," Marcus replied, trying to muster confidence. But deep down, he felt the pressure mounting, and he feared that their bubble of bliss would burst if they weren't careful.

That night, as they shared whispers and stolen kisses, Marcus's thoughts drifted back to Riley's words. The thrill of their love was tempered by the harsh reality of his professional obligations. Each moment with Alex felt precious yet precarious, a balance that could tip at any moment.

As they parted ways, Marcus held Alex's gaze a moment longer, feeling the weight of what lay ahead. "We'll figure it out. I promise," he said, though uncertainty gnawed at the edges of his confidence.

"Just be honest with her," Alex urged, a flicker of worry in his eyes. "The longer we hide, the more chance there is for things to go wrong."

With a heavy heart, Marcus nodded, knowing that Alex was right. The thrill of their secret love affair was intoxicating, but it couldn't last forever without facing the truth. As he walked away, he realized that love was often about risks and choices—and right now, they were standing at a crossroads.

The weight of his hidden life loomed over him like a storm cloud, threatening to overshadow the joy of their connection. As he headed home, he couldn't shake the feeling that the days of hiding in plain sight were numbered. And soon, he would have to confront the reality of their situation or risk losing everything he had come to cherish.

As the days passed, the thrill of their secret affair began to feel less like a romantic escapade and more like a weight bearing down on Alex's conscience. Each stolen moment with Marcus was tinged with a growing sense of unease, as if he were straddling a line that threatened to blur both his personal and professional life. The more he fell for Marcus, the more he grappled with the implications of their relationship.

Sitting at his desk one afternoon, Alex stared blankly at the screen in front of him, a draft of his latest article waiting for his attention. The words blurred together, each sentence morphing into an abstract thought that felt utterly disconnected from reality. He knew he was supposed to be writing about Marcus's impressive stats and upcoming games, but all he could think about were the intimate moments they shared—the laughter, the kisses, the warmth of Marcus's embrace.

Yet every time he wrote, a nagging voice in the back of his mind reminded him of the lies he was telling. The truth of his connection to Marcus loomed like an uninvited guest, pushing against the walls of his carefully constructed facade. How could he continue to feign objectivity when every word he wrote was colored by personal feelings?

With a heavy sigh, he pushed away from his desk, the weight of the dilemma settling deeper into his chest. Alex paced the room, feeling the walls close in around him. He wanted nothing more than to be honest about his relationship with Marcus, but the consequences could be dire. If he revealed their connection, he risked not only his job but also the very thing he cherished most: his bond with Marcus.

Could he bear to lose that? The thought sent a fresh wave of panic coursing through him. Marcus had brought a joy into his life that he hadn't felt in years—a connection that made the chaos of the world fade away. Yet here he was, caught in a web of secrets, feeling trapped between love and career.

As he pulled out his phone, he hesitated. Should he text Marcus and share his fears? Would that only add more pressure to an already complicated situation? Instead, he sent a quick message to his colleague, hoping to distract himself.

"Hey, any news on the next game?"

But as he waited for a response, the silence felt deafening. The anxiety that had been brewing inside him began to bubble over.

That evening, Alex found himself at a local coffee shop, the comforting hum of conversation around him doing little to soothe his mind. He ordered a latte and took a seat by the window, staring out at the bustling street. People walked by, oblivious to the turmoil churning within him.

His thoughts turned to Marcus. He envisioned him on the court, focused and determined, the weight of the world on his shoulders. How was he managing this pressure? Did Marcus feel as trapped as he did? The very idea made Alex's heart ache.

He glanced at his phone, contemplating whether to call Marcus. Their conversations had always been a source of comfort, a way to connect amid the chaos. But what could he say? "Hey, I love you, but I can't keep lying to my paper"? Would that only add to Marcus's burden?

Before he could decide, his phone buzzed, pulling him from his thoughts. It was a message from Marcus:

"Thinking about you. Can we talk later?"

A warmth spread through Alex at the sight of Marcus's name, but it was quickly followed by anxiety. They needed to talk—about the future, about what this all meant.

"Yeah, I'd like that. When?" he typed back, heart racing.

"After the game tonight. Let's meet at the usual spot."

As he read Marcus's response, the knot in his stomach tightened. The "usual spot" had become their sanctuary, a place where they could share their thoughts away from the world. But tonight felt different. Tonight would be about more than just stolen kisses and whispered secrets. It would be about confronting the reality of their relationship.

The evening dragged on as Alex returned home, his mind racing with possibilities and fears. What would he say? How could he express the turmoil he felt without pushing Marcus away?

When he arrived at the alcove, the familiar rush of excitement coursed through him, but it was accompanied by an unsettling tension. Marcus arrived moments later, a look of determination on his face.

"Hey," Marcus greeted, his voice steady yet tinged with concern. "You okay?"

Alex nodded, but the truth lay heavy on his heart. "We need to talk," he said, the gravity of his words hanging in the air.

"Yeah, I know," Marcus replied, his expression serious. "I've been feeling the pressure from Riley. She's asking too many questions, and I don't want to put you in a difficult position."

"I feel trapped, Marcus," Alex confessed, his voice trembling slightly. "I can't keep lying to my paper, but I don't want to lose you. I just don't know what to do."

Marcus stepped closer, his eyes filled with understanding. "We're in a tough spot, but I don't want you to feel like you have to choose. I care about you, and I want us to figure this out together."

The sincerity in Marcus's voice tugged at Alex's heart. It was a comfort amidst the chaos, a reminder that their bond was real. Yet the reality of their situation pressed down on him like a weight.

"I love you, Marcus," Alex said, the words spilling out before he could stop them. "But I can't keep hiding. I need to be honest with my readers, and I don't want to lose everything I've worked for."

Marcus's gaze softened, the tension in his shoulders easing slightly. "I love you too. But we need to figure out how to do this without losing ourselves in the process. Let's talk about our options."

As they stood together in the dim light, the weight of their situation felt both heavy and liberating. Alex knew they had difficult conversations ahead, but in that moment, surrounded by the chaos of the outside world, he felt a glimmer of hope. They were in this together, and maybe—just maybe—they could find a way to navigate the storm while keeping their love intact.

Chapter 5: Close Call

The energy in the air was electric as the high-profile NBA event kicked off, a gathering of fans, players, and media all buzzing with excitement. Alex had been covering these events for years, but this time felt different. He was acutely aware of the stakes involved, especially with Marcus in attendance. The mingling of lights, sounds, and people made it an exhilarating yet daunting experience.

As he navigated through the throngs of fans and reporters, Alex's heart raced—not just from the usual adrenaline of the event, but from the anticipation of seeing Marcus. They had agreed to meet discreetly, but Alex couldn't shake the sense of unease that clung to him.

"Just stay calm," he muttered to himself, trying to push down the anxiety bubbling within him. He scanned the room, looking for Marcus's familiar figure amidst the crowd. When he finally spotted him, a wave of relief washed over him. Marcus was standing by the refreshment table, surrounded by a small group of fans. He looked effortlessly handsome, exuding charisma, but Alex could see the tension etched into his features.

Alex made his way toward him, his pulse quickening as he got closer. Just as he was about to call out to Marcus, a flash of movement caught his eye. It was Riley, Marcus's agent, making her way through the crowd, her sharp gaze surveying the scene like a hawk. The instinct to hide kicked in, and Alex ducked behind a nearby pillar, heart pounding in his chest.

From his vantage point, he could see Marcus laughing with a fan, his smile genuine and infectious. But as Riley approached, Alex's stomach churned. He felt like a deer caught in headlights, frozen in place as he watched the scene unfold. If Riley spotted him with Marcus, their secret would be exposed in an instant.

"Hey, Marcus, great game tonight!" one of the fans said, clapping him on the shoulder.

"Thanks, man! It means a lot," Marcus replied, still smiling, but Alex noticed the flicker of awareness in his eyes. Marcus glanced around, perhaps sensing something amiss.

"Gotta run, but good luck with the season!" the fan added before walking away, leaving Marcus alone at the table just as Riley neared.

Panic surged through Alex. He needed to get out of sight, but he couldn't tear his gaze away. Would Marcus acknowledge him? Would he call out? The seconds felt like hours as he held his breath, waiting for Riley to make her approach.

"Marcus, we need to talk," Riley said, her voice sharp and commanding as she approached him. Alex could see the tension in Marcus's shoulders as he braced himself for the conversation.

"Sure, what's up?" Marcus replied, maintaining his cool demeanor, but Alex could see the flicker of discomfort in his eyes.

"Are you really going to keep dodging my questions? You've been distant lately, and I need to know what's going on," Riley pressed, her voice lowering as she scanned the area.

Alex's heart raced, realizing the risk Marcus was taking by not revealing their relationship. He felt helpless, trapped behind the pillar, wishing he could swoop in and rescue him. But moving now would only draw attention to them both.

Just as Riley turned to look around, Marcus caught Alex's eye and held it for a fleeting moment. There was an unspoken understanding between them, a shared recognition of the danger they were in. It was both thrilling and terrifying, igniting the fire of their connection even in the face of peril.

"Riley, I promise I'm just focusing on my game. I'll be more available, I swear," Marcus replied, his voice steady, though Alex could hear the strain behind the words.

"Marcus, you can't keep playing these games. You're an NBA star; people are watching you. I can't protect you if you don't let me in," Riley insisted, crossing her arms.

Feeling the walls close in, Alex finally made the decision to slip away. He ducked behind another group of fans, moving quietly and quickly, trying to maintain a low profile. Every instinct screamed at him to leave, to protect what they had. He couldn't risk exposure—not now, not when things felt so fragile.

As he maneuvered through the crowd, he couldn't help but steal glances back at Marcus. He wanted nothing more than to reach out, to reassure him, but he knew that could only complicate matters. The uncertainty of the moment pressed down on him, and he could feel the tension in the air, thick and suffocating.

Just as he rounded a corner, he spotted an exit sign glowing faintly ahead. The rush of fresh air felt like a lifeline, and he made his way toward it, heart pounding.

Once outside, Alex leaned against the cool brick wall of the venue, trying to collect his thoughts. The adrenaline was still coursing through him, and he felt a wave of regret wash over him. They had come so close to being caught, and now the reality of their situation felt more precarious than ever.

Minutes later, he felt his phone buzz in his pocket. He pulled it out to see a message from Marcus:

"Are you okay? I didn't see you leave."

"Yeah, I'm outside. Just needed to breathe," Alex replied, his fingers trembling slightly as he typed.

"Riley was asking a lot of questions. I'm sorry you got caught up in that."

"It's not your fault. We just need to be more careful," he sent back, his mind racing with the implications of their close call.

"I don't want to lose you. We'll figure this out," Marcus replied, and Alex could almost feel the weight of his words through the screen.

"I know. Let's meet somewhere else. Somewhere safe."

As he hit send, he took a deep breath, grounding himself in the reality that they were still in this together, despite the chaos surrounding them. The thrill of their love was intoxicating, but it came with risks that they could no longer ignore.

The night had brought them closer to the edge, and Alex knew they needed to take a step back and reevaluate their situation. They were playing a dangerous game, and every close call reminded him that love could be both exhilarating and perilous.

As he waited for Marcus's response, the uncertainty hung in the air like a storm cloud. They had to navigate this carefully, or risk losing everything they had built together.

The aftermath of the event left Alex with a lingering sense of dread. He had hoped the chaos of the evening would fade, but instead, it only amplified the pressure surrounding his relationship with Marcus. As he returned to work the following day, he could feel the weight of secrecy bearing down on him like a lead blanket.

The newsroom buzzed with the typical flurry of activity. Reporters shuffled papers, editors barked orders, and phones rang incessantly. Yet, amid the usual chaos, Alex sensed an unusual tension lingering in the air. He tried to focus on his desk, but his mind kept drifting back to Marcus and the uncertainty of their situation.

It was during the afternoon staff meeting that the storm began to break. Alex sat at the table, his hands clammy, as his editor, Lila, cleared her throat and addressed the room.

"We've received a tip-off about Marcus Greene," Lila announced, her voice steady but laced with intrigue. "There are rumors swirling about his 'mystery man'—someone he's been spotted with multiple times recently."

Alex's heart raced as the words sank in. The whispers were starting to circulate, and he felt a chill creep up his spine. "Mystery man?" he echoed quietly, trying to gauge the reaction around the table.

"Yeah, apparently, he's been seen with someone outside of his usual circle," Lila continued, glancing at her notes. "We need to figure out who this is before the gossip escalates. Alex, I want you to work with the investigative team on this."

A knot tightened in Alex's stomach. The thought of his colleagues digging into Marcus's personal life sent a surge of anxiety through him. "Wait, I—" he started, but Lila cut him off.

"This is important, Alex. We can't let rumors spiral out of control. We need facts," she insisted, her tone brokering no argument.

"Right, of course," he mumbled, feeling trapped. He knew that the investigation would inadvertently put him in the crosshairs, risking exposure of their affair. The last thing he wanted was for his colleagues to uncover the truth behind the 'mystery man.'

As the meeting wrapped up, Alex's mind raced with possibilities. He couldn't let this investigation jeopardize everything he had with Marcus. His thoughts spiraled into panic as he imagined the worst-case scenarios—his relationship exposed, the fallout that would ensue, and the very real threat of losing Marcus.

Over the next few days, Alex threw himself into the investigation, trying to navigate the minefield of rumors while keeping his own secrets close. He and the team sifted through social media posts, scoured gossip columns, and interviewed sources, all while Alex's heart pounded at the thought of someone uncovering the truth.

He found himself frequenting the sidelines of NBA games, cameras flashing and reporters shouting, every moment feeling like a ticking clock. He watched Marcus from afar, observing how the whispers had begun to shift the dynamic around him. The tension was palpable, not just for Alex but for Marcus too, who had begun to look more guarded than ever.

One afternoon, Alex received a text from Marcus that sent his heart racing.

"We need to talk. I'm feeling the pressure from all sides."

"I know. Lila put me on the investigation," Alex replied, dread pooling in his stomach.

"This is getting out of hand. Can we meet tonight?"

"Yes, but we need to be careful."

As he sent the message, a feeling of foreboding settled over him. This was no longer just about their relationship; it was about protecting both their reputations and futures.

That night, they met in a secluded corner of a downtown café, far from prying eyes. As Alex settled into the booth, he watched Marcus walk in, looking like a man carrying the weight of the world on his shoulders. The moment their eyes met, a spark ignited, but it was quickly shadowed by the tension in the air.

"Thanks for meeting me," Marcus said, sliding into the seat across from Alex. His voice was low, edged with anxiety. "I don't know how much longer we can keep this under wraps."

Alex leaned closer, lowering his voice. "I'm doing everything I can, but the rumors are growing. My editor is relentless. She wants to know who the mystery man is, and I'm terrified that I'm going to get caught up in this."

Marcus rubbed his temples, the stress evident in his features. "What if they find out? What will happen to us?"

"I don't know," Alex admitted, the reality hitting him hard. "But I can't lose you. We need to think of a plan. Maybe we should consider being more public—"

"Are you ready for that?" Marcus interrupted, a flash of fear crossing his eyes. "Going public could ruin everything, especially for me. My career..."

"I know, but if we keep hiding, we're only setting ourselves up for a bigger fall," Alex argued, his heart racing. "The longer we stay in the shadows, the more dangerous this becomes."

Marcus leaned back, his expression shifting between hope and despair. "I want to be with you, but the stakes are so high. I'm not just a player; I have a brand to protect. If this gets out..."

The weight of their situation hung heavily between them, and Alex could feel the walls closing in. He reached across the table, taking Marcus's hand in his own. "We'll figure this out. Together. I won't let you down."

As they sat there, hands intertwined, Alex knew the danger was far from over. Gossip had begun to swirl like a tempest, and the pressure was mounting. They were caught in a precarious dance of love and secrecy, and one wrong move could shatter everything they had built.

As they left the café, Alex looked over his shoulder, the feeling of being watched gnawing at him. They were walking a tightrope, and he couldn't shake the feeling that the fall was imminent. All he could do was hold on tight to the fleeting moments they shared and hope they could weather the storm together.

The days following their tense café meeting dragged on, each moment laden with uncertainty. Alex felt the need to protect Marcus, sensing that the walls were closing in around them. The whispers in the media were only getting louder, and he feared that his involvement could be the catalyst for their downfall. So, with a heavy heart, he made the difficult decision to distance himself—at least temporarily.

Late one evening, after an especially challenging day of fielding questions from the investigative team, Alex sat alone in his dimly lit apartment, his mind swirling with conflicting emotions. He knew it was for the best, but the thought of being apart from Marcus sent a pang of sorrow through him. He stared at his phone, contemplating sending a text. But just as he was about to, the screen lit up with a message from Marcus.

"We need to talk. I can't keep doing this."

Alex's heart raced at the urgency of the words. He hesitated, torn between the instinct to protect Marcus and the yearning to see him. Finally, he replied, *"I think it's safer if we don't meet for a while."*

A moment later, the reply came back, sharp and raw. *"You're wrong. I can't let go. I need to see you."*

The determination in Marcus's message ignited a flicker of hope in Alex. Perhaps it was reckless, but he felt the same pull—an emotional gravity that tethered him to Marcus despite the risks. *"Alright. Just be careful. Where should we meet?"*

They settled on a quiet park, a place that had always felt safe and familiar, nestled away from the prying eyes of the world. As night fell, Alex arrived early, pacing beneath the dim glow of the lampposts, heart pounding in anticipation. The cool breeze rustled the leaves overhead, but it did little to calm his nerves.

When Marcus finally appeared, he was dressed in dark jeans and a fitted jacket, his eyes scanning the area with the vigilance of a man who understood the stakes. As their gazes locked, the familiar rush of emotion surged through Alex—a mix of longing, fear, and undeniable love.

"Hey," Marcus said softly, his voice barely above a whisper. He stepped closer, and Alex felt a wave of warmth wash over him, momentarily forgetting the danger they were in.

"Hey," Alex replied, trying to suppress the nervous tremor in his voice. "I'm glad you came."

"I needed to," Marcus said, his brow furrowed in concern. "I don't want to hide anymore, not from you."

As they walked along the gravel path, the world around them faded away. The tension that had lingered in their previous conversations melted into something more profound. With each shared glance, the air crackled with unspoken words, and Alex could feel the intensity of their connection drawing them closer.

They found a secluded bench beneath a canopy of trees, the moonlight filtering through the leaves, casting soft shadows around them. Sitting side by side, the silence stretched, heavy with emotion.

"Alex," Marcus began, his voice low and steady. "I've been thinking about what you said. About being public. I don't want to lose you, and I can't stand the idea of us living in the shadows."

Alex turned to face him, his heart pounding. "I don't want that either, but you know what's at stake. If we go public, it could change everything. Your career, your brand... it's not just about us anymore."

"I get that, but I can't pretend I don't care about you," Marcus said, his eyes shining with vulnerability. "Every moment we're apart feels like a part of me is missing. I refuse to let fear dictate our relationship."

The raw honesty in his words hit Alex like a tidal wave. "Marcus, I feel the same way. But I can't bear the thought of you being hurt because of me."

"I'm willing to take that risk," Marcus insisted, reaching for Alex's hand, his grip firm yet tender. "I want to be with you. All of you. If we have to face the world, let's face it together."

A lump formed in Alex's throat as he absorbed Marcus's words. The love they shared was so powerful, so intoxicating, that it overshadowed the looming threat. "I don't know what that would look like," Alex admitted, his voice trembling slightly.

Marcus leaned in closer, his breath warm against Alex's cheek. "Then let's figure it out together. One step at a time."

In that moment, the air shifted, and Alex felt a wave of emotion wash over him—relief, hope, and a surge of love that drowned out the fear. They both knew the risks, but standing there together, everything else faded away.

Without thinking, Alex closed the distance, their lips crashing together in a passionate kiss that spoke of longing and desperation. The world around them melted away, leaving only the two of them in that shared bubble of connection. It was a kiss fueled by all the emotions they had bottled up—the love, the fear, the thrill of being together despite the odds.

As they pulled away, both breathless, Marcus looked into Alex's eyes, searching for reassurance. "Whatever happens, I want you to know that this is real for me."

"I know," Alex whispered, feeling a swell of emotion rise within him. "And it's real for me too."

They sat in the quiet of the night, their hands intertwined, savoring the moment while knowing the storm still loomed on the horizon. The danger of their situation was real, but in that moment, surrounded by the tranquility of the park, they found solace in each other.

They shared stories, laughter, and unguarded confessions as the night wore on, basking in the warmth of their connection. Time seemed to stretch, allowing them to forget—if only for a little while—the chaos that threatened to engulf them.

But the reality remained: they were dancing on the edge of a cliff, and the wind was picking up. Still, as Alex looked into Marcus's eyes, he felt a flicker of hope that together, they could face whatever came their way.

As they finally stood to leave, Marcus pulled Alex close, his voice a whisper. "No matter what happens, I'm in this for the long haul."

With that, they stepped back into the night, hearts entwined and resolve strengthened. The danger was far from over, but they would face it together, united in a love that could withstand the storm.

Chapter 6: The Threat

The following week was a whirlwind of emotions for Alex and Marcus. They had decided to navigate the tumultuous waters of their relationship together, drawing strength from one another. But just as they began to feel a semblance of normalcy, an ominous shadow fell over their fragile peace.

It was a late afternoon when Marcus received the text. He was lounging on the couch in his apartment, scrolling through social media, when his phone buzzed with a new message. The screen lit up with an unfamiliar number, and curiosity piqued, he opened it.

"I know about you and Alex. It'd be a shame if this got out."

His heart sank, a heavy weight settling in his stomach. The implications were clear, and the threat felt palpable. Who could be behind this? As his mind raced, a chill ran down his spine. The idea of someone exploiting their relationship sent adrenaline coursing through his veins.

Without hesitation, Marcus dialed Alex's number, the ringing echoing in the quiet room. After a few tense moments, Alex answered, his voice bright but quickly shifting to concern when he heard the urgency in Marcus's tone.

"Hey, is everything okay?" Alex asked, sensing the tension.

"No, it's not okay," Marcus replied, his voice tight. "I just got a message that someone knows about us."

"What do you mean, knows?" Alex's heart raced. "Knows what exactly?"

"About our relationship. They sent me a threatening text—something about how it would be a shame if it got out," Marcus said, his words tumbling out in a rush. "I don't know who this is, but I'm scared, Alex."

"Damn," Alex breathed, feeling the gravity of the situation settle over him like a storm cloud. "We have to figure out who could be behind this. Do you have any idea?"

"Not really," Marcus admitted, his voice shaking slightly. "But I've been thinking... it could be someone from the team, maybe even someone in my circle. I've been trying to keep things low-key, but word could have slipped out."

Alex's mind churned with possibilities. "What if it's a journalist? Someone who's been snooping around? You know how cutthroat this industry can be."

"Yeah, that's what I'm afraid of," Marcus replied. "If this gets out, it could destroy everything—not just my career but us too."

They both fell silent for a moment, the weight of the threat looming heavily between them. Alex's mind raced as he tried to think of a plan. "We can't let this intimidate us. Let's investigate quietly. Maybe we can trace the number or find out who else knows about us."

"Good idea," Marcus said, his voice gaining a hint of resolve. "I'll do some digging on my end, see if I can find any leads. Maybe check in with some of my teammates to see if they've heard anything."

"Right," Alex agreed, feeling a surge of determination. "And I'll reach out to some contacts at the paper. Maybe someone's noticed something unusual or heard rumors that could give us a clue."

After hanging up, Alex felt a mix of anxiety and resolve. He was deeply aware of how precarious their situation had become. The relationship that had once felt like a thrilling secret now bore the potential for scandal that could ruin them both.

He spent the rest of the evening combing through his phone contacts and brainstorming possible sources of information. The thought of someone using their relationship against them filled him with anger and fear. They had fought so hard to carve out moments of happiness together, only to be threatened by someone lurking in the shadows.

Later that night, Alex met with his editor, Lila, under the guise of discussing potential articles. He felt the tension in the air as he navigated the conversation carefully, subtly probing for any insight into recent rumors surrounding Marcus.

Lila, however, was focused on the latest developments in the NBA season and the upcoming trades. "I haven't heard anything concrete, but you know how it is. The rumor mill never stops," she said, absentmindedly tapping her pen against her desk.

"Yeah, it's just... I've been hearing some whispers about Marcus," Alex said, testing the waters. "People are curious about his personal life, especially after that close call we had at the event."

Lila raised an eyebrow, intrigued. "Really? Well, you know how players are. They love their privacy. But if there's something brewing, it could make a good story."

Alex swallowed hard, his heart racing at the implications. "Right, but what if it gets twisted? What if someone tries to exploit his personal life for clicks?"

"True, that could be damaging," Lila replied, her expression serious. "But the press isn't the only source of rumors. Players talk. Agents talk. You should be careful, Alex."

The warning echoed in his mind as he left the meeting, anxiety creeping back in. He couldn't shake the feeling that they were being watched, that the threat was closer than he realized.

Later that night, Alex lay in bed, staring at the ceiling, replaying the day's events. He couldn't let this anonymous figure destroy what he and Marcus had built. They needed to stand strong and united, but the looming threat felt like a storm on the horizon—unstoppable and unrelenting.

The next day, Marcus texted him with an update. *"I talked to a few teammates. No one seems to know anything, but there's been some chatter about me being too distracted lately. I don't like it."*

Alex replied, *"We'll figure this out. We have to stay vigilant. We can't let them win."*

As he set his phone down, a sense of determination washed over him. Together, they would confront this threat. They would not be defined by fear, and no one would take away what they had fought so hard to build. But as the reality of their situation sank in, Alex couldn't shake the feeling that the danger was only just beginning.

The days turned into a blur of tension for both Alex and Marcus. The weight of the threat hung over them like a storm cloud, casting a shadow on what had once been a thrilling and passionate connection. Now, every glance and whispered conversation felt loaded with unspoken implications.

As the sun rose on a new day, Alex found himself at the office, but he couldn't shake the feeling of unease that had settled deep within him. The bustling newsroom, usually a sanctuary of creativity and excitement, felt suffocating. He was hyper-aware of his surroundings, constantly glancing over his shoulder, as if the source of their trouble might leap out from the shadows at any moment.

During the morning briefing, Alex struggled to concentrate on the stories being pitched. Instead, his mind was consumed with thoughts of Marcus. He could picture him pacing in his apartment, anxiously wondering if he'd receive another threatening message or if the rumors swirling around the team were gaining traction. The thought made his stomach churn.

When he finally escaped to the break room, he poured himself a cup of coffee, the familiar aroma providing only a momentary distraction from his worries. His colleague Jenna joined him, her expression curious as she leaned against the counter. "You've been looking a little out of it lately, Alex. Everything okay?"

"Yeah, just... busy," he replied, forcing a smile. But inside, the truth weighed heavily on him. The need to protect Marcus felt like a full-time job, and he couldn't shake the anxiety that followed him like a shadow.

Meanwhile, Marcus was in a world of his own, trying to keep a lid on the rumors that were bubbling up among his teammates. He had sensed their curiosity, especially after a couple of late-night absences that had gone unnoticed for too long. The locker room buzzed with whispers, and he could feel the eyes of his peers scrutinizing him, assessing his every move.

At practice, he kept his head down, focusing intently on drills, but the tension was palpable. His friend and teammate, Jake, pulled him aside during a break. "Hey, man, you good? You've been kind of distant lately. Everything okay with you and... you know?"

Marcus forced a laugh, trying to deflect. "Yeah, just a lot on my plate right now. You know how it is with the season ramping up."

Jake studied him for a moment, the concern evident in his eyes. "Look, if something's going on, you can talk to me. You know I've got your back."

"Thanks, I appreciate it," Marcus replied, feeling a pang of guilt at the half-truth. He wanted to confide in Jake, to share the pressure he was under, but the stakes were too high. He couldn't risk anyone else knowing about Alex.

As practice continued, he felt the weight of the world pressing down on him. Each drill seemed more arduous than the last, and every whistle felt like an accusation. Afterward, he retreated to the locker room, hoping for a moment of solitude.

But solitude was elusive. As he undressed, he overheard snippets of conversation from the other players—jokes about dating lives, speculation about who might be "the mystery man" in Marcus's life. The laughter echoed through the room, but it felt sharp and stinging, a reminder of how fragile his situation was.

Marcus's phone buzzed with a text from Alex just as he was about to step into the shower. *"How's it going? You okay?"* The simple message provided a brief comfort, and he quickly replied, *"Just trying to keep things under control. The guys are starting to talk."*

"Stay strong. We'll get through this," Alex responded, and Marcus could almost feel the strength of Alex's resolve through the screen. They were in this together, even if it felt like they were navigating a minefield.

Later that night, when Marcus arrived home, he found himself pacing the floor of his apartment, anxiety coiling in his stomach. He couldn't shake the feeling that someone was watching him, that the threat was closer than he realized. The weight of the text hung over him, an ominous reminder that their relationship was vulnerable.

He decided to call Alex, needing to hear his voice. When Alex answered, the tension in Marcus's chest eased slightly. "Hey, how's it going?"

"Still on edge," Marcus admitted. "I'm worried about the rumors. I don't know how long I can keep deflecting without raising suspicion."

"I get it," Alex said, his tone steady. "But we can't let this ruin what we have. Let's brainstorm some ideas on how to handle it. Maybe I can help with some media strategies from my side."

"Yeah, that could work," Marcus replied, grateful for Alex's unwavering support. "But I need you to be careful too. If they start sniffing around, I can't let you get caught up in this mess."

"I'll be careful," Alex reassured him, though he couldn't shake the feeling that danger was closing in on them both. "We just need to keep communicating. And I'm here for you, always."

As they continued to talk, Marcus felt a flicker of hope amidst the turmoil. They would face this threat together, as partners in every sense of the word. The love they shared was a force that transcended the fear creeping into their lives, and for that, he felt a renewed sense of strength.

But as he hung up, a lingering doubt tugged at him. Would their love be enough to withstand the storm that was brewing? The threat loomed large, and the stakes were higher than ever. They would have to be vigilant and clever, ready to confront whatever came their way. With their relationship hanging in the balance, every decision they made could lead them closer to danger—or toward freedom.

As the days passed, the tension surrounding Alex and Marcus seemed to crystallize into something tangible, a shared weight that they carried together. The threat of exposure loomed larger than ever, but instead of driving them apart, it forged an unbreakable bond between them—one that neither had anticipated but both desperately needed.

One evening, after a particularly grueling day filled with whispered rumors and sidelong glances, Marcus invited Alex over to his apartment. The sun was setting, casting a warm glow across the living room, and for a moment, it felt like they could escape the chaos outside. The air buzzed with an energy that felt both comforting and electric, a cocoon of safety in an otherwise tumultuous time.

They settled onto the couch, the soft fabric a stark contrast to the hard truths they'd been grappling with. As they talked, Marcus opened up in a way he hadn't before, vulnerability spilling out in the quiet spaces between their laughter and shared glances.

"Alex," he began, his voice low and earnest, "I've never felt this way about anyone before. You make me feel... seen. Not just as an athlete, but as a person." His gaze was intense, piercing through the noise of the outside world.

The sincerity in his words tugged at Alex's heart, a rush of warmth spreading through him. "I feel the same way, Marcus. But..." The hesitation hung between them, heavy with implications. "I can't help but think that my involvement could jeopardize your career. This is a risky situation."

Marcus shifted closer, his expression softening. "I understand the risks, believe me. But I can't pretend that what we have isn't real. It's terrifying, but it's also the most real thing I've ever experienced." He reached for Alex's hand, intertwining their fingers, a gesture that spoke volumes more than words could convey.

The warmth of Marcus's skin against his sent a jolt of electricity through Alex, momentarily distracting him from the storm of guilt swirling in his mind. "But what if this blows up? What if it affects your reputation? Your career?"

Marcus shook his head, determination etched across his features. "I can handle the pressure. What I can't handle is losing you. The thought of walking away from this—us—because of fear? That's worse than any rumor or threat."

Alex's heart raced as he absorbed Marcus's words, feeling the weight of the world shifting. "You really mean that?" he asked, searching Marcus's eyes for reassurance.

"Absolutely. I've been living in a world of expectations for so long, but with you, I feel like I can breathe. You're my escape," Marcus confessed, his vulnerability raw and palpable. "I don't want to hide anymore."

But as Alex stared into Marcus's earnest eyes, a dark cloud of doubt settled in the pit of his stomach. Could he really allow himself to be a source of turmoil in Marcus's life? The professional risks loomed large, and the thought of sacrificing Marcus's dreams for the sake of their relationship made his heart ache.

"I want to be with you, Marcus. But I can't shake this feeling that I'm putting you at risk. I can't be the reason you lose everything you've worked for," Alex said, his voice strained.

"You're not a risk; you're my refuge," Marcus replied, his grip on Alex's hand tightening. "We'll navigate this together. I refuse to let anyone dictate how I feel or who I love."

In that moment, Alex felt the tension ease, if only slightly. Marcus's confidence wrapped around him like a shield, and he couldn't help but lean into it. They were facing an uncertain future, but in the face of the looming threat, they were also discovering something extraordinary.

As they leaned in closer, their foreheads nearly touching, the air crackled with unsaid promises. It felt like a declaration of war against the challenges ahead—a vow that they would face whatever came together, no matter the cost.

But in the back of Alex's mind lingered the shadows of doubt. The stakes were high, and the very foundation of their relationship was being tested. Could they withstand the scrutiny? The rumors? The fear of losing each other amidst the chaos?

Despite the turmoil swirling around them, in that intimate moment, all that mattered was their connection. They had each other, and for now, that felt like enough to hold back the darkness.

As they shared a soft kiss, sealing their promise to one another, Alex vowed silently to protect Marcus at all costs. They would fight against the challenges, navigating the treacherous waters together. The bond between them was deepening, and as they pulled away, it was clear that whatever threats lay ahead, they would face them united.

But the question loomed, heavy in the air: would love be enough to shield them from the dangers that lurked just beyond the horizon?

Chapter 7: Desperate Measures

The atmosphere in the newsroom was thick with tension, a palpable pressure that seemed to press down on Alex's shoulders with every passing day. With whispers about Marcus swirling through the media, the urgency for a more revealing story intensified. Alex's editor, Karen, was relentless, her expectations rising as the stakes climbed higher.

"Alex, we need something more—something personal," Karen urged during their morning meeting, her eyes narrowing with determination. "People want to know who Marcus Greene really is beyond the court. Give me the insight that will blow this story wide open. You're in a unique position to provide that."

As Karen's words echoed in his mind, a sense of dread coiled around Alex's heart. He had spent weeks building a fragile bond with Marcus, an intimate connection rooted in trust and understanding. The idea of compromising that trust for the sake of a story felt like treachery. Yet here was Karen, insisting he dig deeper, risking everything he'd built for a sensational headline.

"I understand, but Marcus is a private person," Alex replied, trying to maintain his composure. "He's not just a subject; he's a person. I don't want to exploit his vulnerabilities."

Karen leaned forward, her tone shifting to a more persuasive pitch. "I get that, but if you don't provide more depth, someone else will. The media is buzzing about his 'mystery man,' and if we don't break the story, it could end up in the hands of our competitors. You know how the game works."

The reality of the situation settled heavily on Alex. He felt the tightrope he was walking grow increasingly precarious. On one side was his commitment to Marcus, to protect him and keep their relationship shielded from prying eyes. On the other was his career—a chance to make a name for himself in sports journalism that he had long dreamed of achieving.

As the meeting wrapped up, Alex returned to his desk, his mind racing. He opened his laptop but found it impossible to focus on the article in front of him. Thoughts of Marcus flooded his mind: the way his eyes lit up when he talked about basketball, the vulnerability he had shared in moments of quiet intimacy. How could he betray that by delving into the more sensational aspects of his life?

His phone buzzed with a text from Marcus, breaking through the whirlwind of his thoughts. *"How's the article coming? I miss you."* The message tugged at Alex's heart, grounding him in the reality of their relationship.

"I miss you too. Just dealing with some pressure from the editor," Alex replied, his fingers hovering over the keys as he wrestled with his next thoughts. *"I don't want to compromise you."*

Marcus's response was almost immediate. *"You need to do what's right for you, but don't lose yourself in this. We both knew it would be challenging."*

Alex sighed, feeling the weight of his decision bearing down on him. He wanted to confide in Marcus, to share the turmoil that was swirling inside him. But he also recognized the risk of doing so. Would talking about the pressure jeopardize Marcus's peace of mind? Would it make him feel like he was dragging Alex into his troubles?

As the hours passed, Alex's mind continued to spiral. He replayed every moment they had spent together, every intimate conversation that had solidified their bond. The image of Marcus, filled with passion and intensity, contrasted sharply with the cutthroat world of journalism. How could he reconcile the two?

Later that evening, he received another message from Marcus, this one filled with warmth and a hint of vulnerability. *"Let's meet tonight. I want to see you."*

Alex's heart raced at the thought of being with Marcus, but he hesitated. He had to come clean about the pressure he was facing, but he feared that sharing this would introduce unnecessary stress into their already precarious relationship.

After a moment of contemplation, he replied, *"Okay. I'll be there."*

When he arrived at Marcus's apartment, he found the door slightly ajar, the soft glow of lights spilling into the hallway. As he stepped inside, the scent of Marcus's cologne wrapped around him, an immediate comfort amidst the chaos of his thoughts.

Marcus was waiting in the living room, a smile breaking across his face as he saw Alex. The warmth of the moment enveloped him, but as Alex stepped closer, the weight of the conversation he needed to have loomed overhead.

"Hey, you," Marcus said, pulling him into an embrace. "I've missed you."

"I missed you too," Alex replied, allowing himself to relax for a moment in Marcus's presence. But the smile faded as he steeled himself for the truth he needed to share. "We need to talk."

Marcus's expression shifted slightly, concern flickering in his eyes. "What's on your mind?"

Taking a deep breath, Alex plunged into the depths of his struggle. "Karen wants more personal insights into your life for the article. She's pushing me to dig deeper, and I don't know how to handle it without compromising you."

Marcus's gaze darkened, the reality of the situation settling heavily between them. "I get it. This is a tough position for you. But you have to do what you feel is right. If this is about my life, I don't want you to sacrifice your career or integrity for me."

"I don't want to exploit you," Alex said, desperation creeping into his voice. "But I also don't want to lose this opportunity. It feels like I'm caught in the middle of two worlds, and I don't know how to balance them."

The silence hung between them, thick and uncomfortable. Marcus stepped closer, his eyes piercing into Alex's, searching for understanding. "You're not just a journalist; you're my partner. Whatever you decide, I trust you. But please, just be honest with me. I can handle the truth."

With Marcus's words echoing in his heart, Alex felt a glimmer of clarity. In that moment, he realized that no career achievement was worth sacrificing the bond they had forged. He would figure out a way to navigate this challenge without losing sight of what mattered most.

"Okay," Alex finally said, resolve building within him. "I'll find a way to balance it. But we'll face this together. I promise."

Marcus's smile returned, lighting up the room. "Together."

In that shared promise, amidst the tumult of their lives, they found a renewed sense of strength. They were navigating uncharted waters, but together they could withstand any storm that came their way. The love they shared would be their anchor, no matter the challenges that lay ahead.

The mood shifted in Marcus's apartment as the reality of their situation settled heavily on both men. After sharing their concerns, the atmosphere thickened with unspoken fears, and it felt as if they were standing on the precipice of a decision that could change everything.

"Maybe we should just come clean," Marcus suggested, his voice steady but tinged with urgency. "If we go public, we can control the narrative. We can own our truth."

Alex's heart raced at the thought, but an icy wave of apprehension washed over him. "You know how the media works, Marcus. They won't just report our story—they'll sensationalize it. They'll turn your career into a spectacle. This isn't just about us; it's about your entire future."

Marcus's brow furrowed as he paced the small living room, his agitation palpable. "But if we keep hiding, it's only a matter of time before someone finds out. The whispers are already starting. You saw the rumors—'the mystery man.' How long do you think we can keep this under wraps?"

Alex stood his ground, frustration bubbling beneath the surface. "I know that! But what if it backfires? What if your team decides you're a liability? You've worked so hard to get where you are; I can't bear the thought of jeopardizing everything for the sake of our relationship."

"Are you saying I should just pretend this doesn't matter?" Marcus shot back, his voice rising. "I won't hide who I am or who I love! I refuse to live in the shadows because I'm afraid of what people might think!"

The intensity of their argument hung in the air, charged and electric. Alex felt his own anger flare. "It's not just about fear, Marcus! It's about reality! Your career isn't just a job; it's your life's work! You're a public figure, and this kind of revelation can have devastating consequences!"

"Are you prioritizing my career over our relationship?" Marcus challenged, crossing his arms defensively. "Because it sure feels like you are!"

The accusation struck a nerve, and Alex's heart sank. "That's not fair. You know that's not what I mean. I care about you—about us! But I also care about the risks involved. I want you to be successful. I don't want to be the reason you fall from grace."

Marcus's expression softened momentarily, the anger giving way to a mix of frustration and vulnerability. "You're not just a journalist to me, Alex. You're someone I love. How can we build something real if we're always looking over our shoulders? If we're always afraid?"

Torn between his love for Marcus and the harsh realities of the world they inhabited, Alex took a deep breath, trying to find a way to articulate his feelings. "I'm not saying we should hide forever. But maybe we need to wait until the time is right? Until we know how to protect you? I don't want to rush into something that could ruin everything for you."

Marcus turned away, running a hand through his hair in frustration. "I hate feeling like I'm living a lie. I'm tired of pretending to be someone I'm not. I want to be with you openly, without fear or shame."

The vulnerability in Marcus's voice tugged at Alex's heart, and he stepped closer, placing a hand on Marcus's shoulder. "I want that too. More than anything. But the world we live in doesn't make it easy for people like us. It's a dangerous game."

For a moment, silence fell between them, each lost in their own thoughts. The weight of their argument lingered, creating an uncomfortable tension that neither wanted to ignore. Finally, Marcus sighed, looking out the window as if seeking clarity in the darkness.

"What do you want, Alex?" he asked, his voice quiet. "What do you truly want?"

Alex's heart raced as he contemplated the question. The answer was complicated, layered with fear, hope, and love. "I want you, Marcus. I want us. But I also want you to succeed and be happy. I don't want my feelings to hold you back."

Marcus turned to face him, searching Alex's eyes for sincerity. "Then we need to find a way to navigate this together. I can't do it alone. If we decide to stay private for now, let's at least have a plan. A strategy for when we're ready to face the world."

The idea resonated with Alex, offering a glimmer of hope amidst the chaos. "A plan sounds good. But it has to be something we both agree on, something that puts your career first. I want to support you, not put you at risk."

Marcus nodded, the anger in his eyes softening as he recognized the truth in Alex's words. "Okay. We'll take it one step at a time. But we can't keep living in fear. We need to make sure we have a future, not just for us, but for the life you deserve."

Alex felt a wave of relief wash over him, knowing they were both willing to compromise. "Let's be strategic, then. We'll lay low, but we'll also keep an open line of communication about how we're feeling. If we're ever in danger of being exposed, we'll figure out a way to handle it."

As Marcus reached out, taking Alex's hand in his, a sense of unity settled between them. They were navigating uncharted waters, but they would do so together, facing the challenges as a team.

"I love you, Alex," Marcus said softly, squeezing his hand. "And whatever happens, I'm grateful for you. We'll find our way through this."

With those words, a renewed sense of determination washed over Alex. They were committed to each other, and while the future remained uncertain, their love would be the anchor that guided them through the storm. Together, they would face the world on their terms, navigating the delicate balance of love and ambition, each step drawing them closer to a future they both longed for.

The atmosphere in Marcus's apartment shifted once more, the remnants of their heated argument fading into a shared resolve. The weight of their earlier words lingered in the air, but instead of creating a chasm between them, it forged a deeper understanding. They were both standing at the crossroads of love and ambition, and it was time to choose their path.

As the silence settled, Alex watched Marcus's expression evolve from frustration to determination. It was clear that both men were ready to lay aside their fears and confront the reality of their situation.

"Let's not forget why we're in this together," Marcus said, his voice steady as he turned to face Alex fully. "We care about each other. That should come first, no matter what the world throws at us. I won't let fear dictate our relationship."

Alex felt a surge of warmth at Marcus's words. "You're right. We can't let external pressures tear us apart. I love you, and I want to fight for us, not against each other."

Marcus stepped closer, their bodies mere inches apart, a magnetism drawing them together. "So, what's the plan? How do we move forward?"

Alex considered the question, the possibilities racing through his mind. "We keep things low-key for now, but we don't shut ourselves off completely. Let's be honest about what we're feeling and what we want. If the rumors get worse, we address them together."

Marcus nodded, a small smile breaking through the tension. "I like that. No more hiding in the shadows. We'll live our lives, and if people ask questions, we'll tackle them head-on. We deserve that freedom."

The idea of living authentically, even with the potential for exposure, resonated deeply with Alex. "Together, we can handle whatever comes our way. We'll protect each other. But if it gets too risky, we'll have to be smart about our choices."

"Agreed," Marcus said, his voice low yet filled with conviction. "If we're going to do this, we need to be all in. No more half-measures."

The intensity of the moment electrified the air between them. As if sensing the shift, Marcus took a step closer, his gaze unwavering. "I want to be with you, Alex. I want to share my life with you openly. I'm ready to take that risk."

"Then let's do it," Alex replied, a mixture of excitement and fear coursing through him. "Let's be honest about who we are, and if we face backlash, we'll deal with it together."

The resolve settled between them like a protective shield. It was a promise of solidarity, of partnership in the face of adversity. They were no longer just two men entangled in a secret; they were a team willing to confront the world, no matter the cost.

In that moment, the air shifted from uncertainty to possibility. Alex stepped forward, his heart racing as he wrapped his arms around Marcus, pulling him close. "I love you, and I don't want to lose you. Whatever happens, we'll face it together."

"I love you too, Alex," Marcus murmured against Alex's shoulder, the warmth of his body anchoring Alex's resolve. "Together. Always."

Their embrace tightened, and in that safe cocoon, they felt the world outside fade away. The worries of their lives, the pressures from the media, and the fears of exposure all felt distant in that moment. All that mattered was their love, stronger than the challenges they faced.

As they finally pulled back to look into each other's eyes, the intensity of their connection was unmistakable. They were bound by something deeper than fear; they were bonded by love and a shared commitment to fight for what they cherished.

"Let's make a pact," Marcus said, a determined glint in his eyes. "Whatever comes our way, we promise to communicate openly. No more secrets between us, even if it's hard."

"I promise," Alex said, his heart swelling with admiration. "We'll navigate this together, one step at a time."

With their pact solidified, they found comfort in the strength of their union. Outside the world continued to spin, but within those walls, they had created a sanctuary where love triumphed over fear.

As the evening deepened, they shared their dreams and hopes, envisioning a future that embraced both their passions—Marcus's career and Alex's journalistic integrity. Each word exchanged solidified their commitment to one another, transforming their love into a force that could withstand any storm.

In that moment, Alex realized that love was not just about the grand gestures or the perfect moments; it was about standing firm together, facing challenges with unwavering resolve. They would be each other's advocates, allies, and partners, even in the face of uncertainty.

The night wore on, filled with laughter, shared stories, and plans for what lay ahead. With every passing minute, their fears began to dissipate, replaced by the promise of a future they could build together. They had decided to embrace their truth, no matter the consequences, and that choice brought them closer than ever before.

As they settled into each other's arms, Alex felt an overwhelming sense of peace wash over him. The journey ahead might be fraught with obstacles, but he knew that together they could conquer anything. Love was their greatest strength, and they were ready to face whatever came next—together.

Chapter 8: Exposed

The day began like any other for Alex, filled with the usual whirlwind of deadlines, interviews, and the chaos of the sports world. He was sitting in his small office, pouring over notes for his next piece on Marcus when the phone call came in. It was his editor, Matt, a voice that usually brought either reassurance or tension. But today, it was something much more unsettling.

"Alex, can you come to my office? We need to talk," Matt said, his tone clipped and serious.

A knot tightened in Alex's stomach as he made his way down the corridor, the hum of the newsroom around him fading into an ominous silence. He couldn't shake the feeling that something was off. Had someone discovered his secret with Marcus? The thought raced through his mind, igniting a mix of anxiety and dread.

When he reached Matt's office, he found the door ajar. Stepping inside, he was met with the sight of his editor leaning back in his chair, a look of intrigue dancing across his features. "Have a seat," Matt said, gesturing toward the chair opposite him.

Alex sat, feeling the tension coiling in his chest. "What's going on?"

Matt's gaze sharpened, his expression shifting from casual to serious. "I received a tip-off this morning. Someone in the industry mentioned they've seen you and Marcus together, and it seems our little secret isn't as secret as we thought."

Alex's heart raced, a surge of anger and panic coursing through him. "You mean someone knows? Who?"

"Doesn't matter right now," Matt replied, leaning forward, a glint of something uncomfortably opportunistic in his eyes. "What matters is the potential here. You've got a unique story, Alex—one that could bring in major views and readership for the paper."

Alex felt his stomach drop. "You're not suggesting what I think you are."

"I'm saying I want you to write it," Matt said, his voice low and conspiratorial. "Your perspective. Your experience with Marcus. This could be the story of the year, and you're in a prime position to tell it."

Fury ignited within Alex, a wildfire consuming his rational thoughts. "You want me to exploit my relationship with Marcus? That's what this is about? You're willing to throw me into the spotlight like a sacrificial lamb?"

Matt raised his hands in a defensive gesture. "I'm not throwing you to the wolves, Alex. Think about the opportunity! This is a chance to define your career. You could be the go-to journalist on this story."

"Define my career?" Alex echoed incredulously, disbelief lacing his voice. "You mean you want me to betray the one person I care about? You want me to put Marcus in danger for a headline?"

The air in the room grew thick with tension, Matt's expression hardening. "This isn't just about you and Marcus anymore. This is a business. If you don't take this opportunity, someone else will. You could be the one breaking the story, not just the one being caught up in it."

Alex clenched his fists, anger surging through him. "I can't believe this. I trusted you to respect my integrity as a journalist. Instead, you want me to sell out the person I love. This is beyond unethical."

"Think about your career, Alex! You've been trying to make a name for yourself for years. This is it. This could be your big break," Matt pressed, his tone shifting from persuasive to demanding.

"No," Alex said, shaking his head vehemently. "I won't do it. I refuse to put Marcus's life and career at risk for a story. This isn't just journalism; it's personal, and I won't be part of that."

The silence between them was palpable, a chasm formed by differing values and priorities. Alex's heart was pounding, the weight of his emotions pressing down on him like a vice.

Matt leaned back, crossing his arms, a calculated expression on his face. "So, what's your plan? To keep this under wraps indefinitely? Because if you think that's going to work, you're delusional. The clock is ticking, Alex."

"I don't care," Alex replied defiantly, his voice firm. "I won't sacrifice Marcus for this paper or for my career. If you publish anything about me or him, I'll walk. I won't be complicit in this betrayal."

Matt's expression hardened, the air growing charged with unspoken tensions. "You think you can just walk away? This is bigger than you, and you know it. I suggest you reconsider."

With that, Alex stood, heart racing with anger and disappointment. He couldn't believe he was in this position, forced to choose between his career and the man he loved.

"You know what? I don't want to be part of a paper that operates like this. I thought I could trust you."

As he turned to leave, Matt called after him, frustration lacing his voice. "This isn't just a personal matter, Alex! You're being naive! You need to see the bigger picture!"

But Alex was already out the door, his heart pounding with a mix of betrayal and determination. He couldn't believe the lengths to which his editor was willing to go for a story. As he walked down the corridor, he felt the weight of the decision he had to make hanging heavy over him.

In that moment, the world felt darker, and the future seemed uncertain. He had to protect Marcus at all costs, even if it meant sacrificing his own ambitions. Their love was worth more than any story, and he was ready to fight for it.

As he left the office, Alex's mind raced with thoughts of how to approach Marcus. He needed to talk to him, to explain what had happened and how they could navigate this new threat together. The danger was real, and they were both at risk of being exposed.

But despite the fear clawing at him, Alex felt a renewed sense of purpose. No matter what happened next, he would stand by Marcus's side. They would face the fallout together, because in the end, love was the most important story worth telling.

The morning after Alex's confrontation with Matt, the tension in the air was palpable. Alex sat in his apartment, coffee untouched as he scrolled through his phone, dread tightening in his chest with every headline he saw. News outlets buzzed with rumors about Marcus's personal life, each article more sensational than the last. Phrases like "NBA Star's Secret

Affair" and "Mystery Man Revealed" jumped out at him, each click revealing more details that felt invasive and cruel.

A knot twisted in Alex's stomach. He had hoped to keep their relationship shielded from prying eyes a little longer, but now it felt like the walls were closing in. The leak had come like a storm, unexpected and ruthless, leaving chaos in its wake.

His phone buzzed, a text from Marcus flashing across the screen. *Can we meet? I need to talk.*

The urgency in the message sent a rush of concern through Alex. He quickly typed back, *Of course. Where?*

My place. Half an hour?

As he gathered himself to leave, his mind raced with worry. He couldn't shake the feeling that this would be a pivotal moment for both of them.

When Alex arrived at Marcus's apartment, he found the star athlete pacing the living room, his expression a mix of frustration and determination. Marcus looked up, relief washing over his features when he saw Alex, but it was short-lived. The weight of the situation loomed heavy between them.

"Did you see the news?" Marcus asked, running a hand through his hair in frustration.

Alex nodded, his heart aching at the sight of Marcus so visibly affected. "I did. I'm so sorry, Marcus. I never wanted this to happen."

Marcus let out a deep breath, shaking his head as he gestured for Alex to sit. "I can't believe this. It's all over the place. My team is in a frenzy, trying to manage the fallout."

"What are they saying?" Alex asked, bracing himself for the worst.

"They want to spin it. They're suggesting a cover story—something about me being focused on my career and not having time for relationships." Marcus paused, the turmoil in his eyes evident. "They think it'll protect my image."

Alex felt a surge of anger. "But that's a lie. You shouldn't have to hide who you are or who you love. This is your life, Marcus."

"I know," Marcus said, his voice strained. "But they're right about one thing: my career is on the line. If I don't handle this carefully, it could ruin everything I've worked for."

"Have you thought about what you want?" Alex asked, urgency creeping into his tone. "What does honesty mean for you?"

"I want to be honest with myself," Marcus replied, his voice firm despite the tremor in it. "I refuse to live a lie. I'm not going to pretend like I'm not in love with you. That's not who I am."

Alex's heart swelled at his words, but the reality of the situation loomed large. "But if you refuse to play along, it could cost you everything—the endorsements, the contracts… everything you've built."

"Maybe it's time for a different approach," Marcus said, his determination shining through the worry. "I want to own my truth. I'm tired of being told how to live my life. If they can't accept who I am, then maybe I don't need to work with them."

The fierce resolve in Marcus's eyes gave Alex pause. It was clear that this was more than just a professional dilemma; it was a deeply personal one. "You really mean that, don't you? You want to go public about us?"

"Absolutely," Marcus said, his voice steady. "I want to live my life openly, not in fear. I'm done hiding. I want to be with you, and I won't let anyone dictate how I do that."

Alex felt a rush of admiration for Marcus, the bravery in his stance igniting a fire within him. "I want that too. But we need to be prepared for the backlash. It won't be easy."

"I'm ready for it," Marcus replied, a fierce light in his eyes. "I'd rather face the world together than live in secrecy. I want to own my narrative, not let someone else write it for me."

A weight lifted slightly from Alex's chest as he absorbed Marcus's words. It was a risky decision, one that could change everything. But in that moment, he felt the same resolve swelling within him.

"Then we'll do it together," Alex said firmly. "We'll face whatever comes our way. No more hiding."

As they locked eyes, the unspoken promise hung between them, a commitment to navigate the challenges ahead. They were no longer just two people caught in a whirlwind of circumstances; they were partners ready to stand together in the face of adversity.

"Let's prepare for the fallout," Marcus said, a hint of determination in his tone. "We can't control how people will react, but we can control our response. We'll be honest, and we'll support each other through whatever comes next."

"Absolutely," Alex agreed, his heart racing with both fear and exhilaration. "Let's take charge of this. We'll show the world who we are, and we won't let anyone tear us apart."

They spent the next hour strategizing, outlining how to manage the incoming media storm while also preparing for the emotional toll it would take on both of them. Each word shared felt like a foundation being laid for a future that, while uncertain, was undeniably theirs.

As Alex left Marcus's apartment, the weight of the world still pressed down on them, but now it felt like a weight they could share. Together, they would face the exposure, the rumors, and the challenges, united in their truth.

In that moment, Alex knew that love wasn't just about the good times; it was about standing firm when the world threatened to pull them apart. And as they took their first steps into the light, he felt a surge of hope. No matter what lay ahead, they would face it side by side, ready to fight for their love and for the authenticity that had brought them together in the first place.

The following week was a whirlwind of media frenzy and speculation, with news outlets dissecting every nuance of Marcus Greene's life. Alex had watched from the sidelines, anxiety creeping in with each article that popped up on his phone. But amidst the chaos, he could feel the determination radiating from Marcus. They were in this together, and Marcus was ready to take the next step.

The day arrived when Marcus would address the rumors publicly. It was a press conference unlike any he'd held before—one not just about his performance on the court, but about his life off it. Alex sat in the front row, heart pounding with anticipation. This was the moment they had both been preparing for, and the tension in the air was electric.

As Marcus walked onto the stage, he exuded confidence, his tall frame radiating a mixture of strength and vulnerability. The media was buzzing, cameras flashing, and microphones being thrust toward him as he took his seat at the podium. Alex held his breath, his palms clammy with nerves.

"Thank you all for being here," Marcus began, his voice steady. "I know there's been a lot of talk recently about my personal life. I want to take a moment to address it."

A wave of silence fell over the room, all eyes glued to him, waiting for the revelation.

"I've always believed in honesty," he continued, his gaze sweeping over the crowd. "As a public figure, I've shared much of my journey with you—the victories, the struggles, the sacrifices. But there's one part of my life I've kept private, something I've been afraid to share."

Alex's heart raced as he listened. This was it—the moment when Marcus would finally reveal the truth, or at least part of it.

"I've been fortunate to find meaningful connections in my life," Marcus said, pausing as if weighing his words carefully. "And while I've always prioritized my career, I want to acknowledge that there's someone special who has brought a lot of joy into my life. Someone who sees me for who I truly am, beyond the basketball court."

Gasps and whispers rippled through the crowd, the energy shifting as the media tried to process his words. Marcus continued, his voice unwavering. "I know that the world can be quick to judge and speculate. But I want to remind everyone that there's more to me than just my stats and highlights. I am a person, with feelings, hopes, and dreams—just like you."

As he spoke, Alex felt a mix of pride and fear. Marcus was hinting at the truth without fully revealing it, leaving a tantalizing thread for the media and fans to unravel. It was a clever move, acknowledging the relationship while maintaining a level of privacy.

Marcus's eyes softened as he continued, "I believe in being true to myself, and I hope that by sharing this, I can encourage others to do the same. Life is too short to hide who you are or who you love."

The room erupted into applause, but Alex could hear the chatter beginning—questions and speculations buzzing about who this special person could be. Despite the uncertainty, Marcus's words resonated deeply. He was taking a stand, one that would ripple through the NBA and beyond.

As the press conference came to a close, Marcus smiled, his eyes scanning the room before landing on Alex. In that brief moment, the connection between them was palpable, a silent understanding of the risks they were both taking. He had chosen authenticity over silence, and it was both exhilarating and terrifying.

After the event, Alex was flooded with messages from colleagues and friends. The speculation was rampant; social media was ablaze with guesses and theories about Marcus's "mystery man." Yet, amidst the chaos, Alex felt a sense of relief wash over him. They had taken a bold step together, and no matter how the world reacted, they had each other.

When Alex finally reached Marcus backstage, the air was charged with energy. Marcus looked both exhilarated and exhausted, a small smile tugging at his lips.

"You did it," Alex said, his voice filled with admiration. "You were incredible."

"I was terrified," Marcus admitted, running a hand through his hair. "But I knew it was time. I couldn't hide anymore. It felt good to say those things."

Alex stepped closer, wrapping his arms around Marcus in a tight embrace. "I'm so proud of you. You were brave, and you showed everyone who you are."

They pulled back slightly, their foreheads touching, sharing a moment of intimacy amidst the whirlwind of chaos. "But now what?" Marcus asked, concern flickering in his eyes. "The media is going to go wild with this. We're not out of the woods yet."

"I know," Alex replied, determination setting in. "But whatever happens, we'll face it together. We'll navigate this storm side by side."

Marcus nodded, the strength of their bond evident in the way he held Alex's gaze. "Together," he echoed, a promise resonating in those simple words.

As they stepped out of the backstage area, the sounds of the media frenzy filled the air. Cameras flashed, voices clamored for attention, but this time, Alex felt a new sense of purpose. They were no longer hiding in the shadows; they were stepping into the light, ready to confront whatever came their way.

Hand in hand, they faced the buzz of the world outside, knowing that their love—once a secret—was now a force that could not be ignored. The road ahead would be challenging, but they were prepared to tackle it head-on, united in their truth and their unwavering commitment to each other.

Chapter 9: The Fallout

The aftermath of Marcus's press conference was immediate and overwhelming. What had started as a courageous step towards honesty had turned into a whirlwind of backlash that neither of them had fully anticipated.

As news outlets dove deeper into Marcus's personal life, social media erupted with mixed reactions. Some fans celebrated his bravery, rallying around him as a beacon of authenticity, while others condemned him for his choices, questioning his commitment to the game and his status as a role model. The juxtaposition was stark, and the noise was deafening.

Alex felt the brunt of the fallout in a different way. His editor at the paper had called him into the office the day after the announcement, a tense expression etched across her face. "We need to talk," she said, gesturing for him to sit.

"What's going on?" Alex asked, anxiety prickling at his skin. He already sensed that things were shifting.

"It's about your piece on Marcus," she began, folding her arms. "The angle you took—while I understand the sentiment behind it—has not gone over well with the upper management."

Alex's heart sank. "What do you mean? I was just trying to tell the truth."

"The truth is one thing," she replied, her tone sharp. "But you've crossed a line between journalist and participant. This isn't just a story anymore; it's personal. Management is concerned that you're too close to the subject, and they think it's affecting your objectivity."

"So, what? You're going to bury my piece?" Alex shot back, frustration bubbling to the surface.

"They want to distance the paper from the relationship. We can't afford to lose sponsorships or credibility because of personal connections," she explained, her voice softening slightly. "They're reconsidering your position on the sports beat. You might be reassigned."

Anger coursed through Alex. "You're going to throw me under the bus because I care about someone? That's not fair!"

"I'm trying to protect you," she replied, but the sincerity in her tone did little to alleviate his anger. "You need to understand how this looks from a business perspective."

As he left the meeting, Alex felt a sense of dread settle in. He knew the road ahead would be rocky, and with Marcus facing his own set of challenges, the weight of it all felt crushing.

Meanwhile, Marcus was navigating his own storm. Sponsorships began to pull back, citing a need to maintain a "clean image" amid the unfolding scandal. His agent, who had been a steady force in his career, now seemed more like a worried parent, urging him to issue a statement reaffirming his commitment to the game and downplaying the relationship.

"Marcus, we need to think about your brand," his agent insisted during a tense phone call. "This is bigger than you realize. You can't let this define you."

"I won't apologize for who I love," Marcus shot back, his voice steady but laced with frustration. "I refuse to compromise my integrity for endorsements."

"Then be prepared for the consequences," the agent warned, the line going silent for a moment. "This could affect your entire career."

Despite the weight of the conversation, Marcus felt a sense of clarity. He wouldn't let fear dictate his life. That resolve carried him through the initial wave of backlash, but it didn't make the toll any lighter.

Alex and Marcus leaned on each other as they processed the fallout, their evenings spent in quiet companionship, sharing meals, and watching mindless TV. They talked about everything—how the world was reacting, their fears for the future, and the love that kept pulling them closer despite the chaos surrounding them.

One evening, as they sat on Marcus's couch, the silence grew heavy. "Do you think we made a mistake?" Marcus asked quietly, his eyes fixed on the television screen but not really seeing it.

"No," Alex replied firmly. "We did what we needed to do. But the world isn't ready for it, and that's not our fault."

Marcus sighed, leaning back against the cushions. "I just hate that this is impacting your career too. You've worked so hard."

"More than anything, I hate that we're both suffering for simply being ourselves," Alex said, his voice filled with empathy. "But we'll get through this together. We'll find a way to navigate it, no matter how tough it gets."

Despite their shared determination, the stress was evident in their interactions. Moments that had once been filled with laughter and ease now felt laden with uncertainty. They both struggled to maintain a sense of normalcy amid the storm.

Marcus received an outpouring of messages from fans—some supportive, others scathing. "I can't believe you'd choose a man over your career," one message read, while another celebrated him as a role model. The conflicting sentiments played on his mind, weighing heavily on his heart.

Alex, too, faced questions from friends and colleagues. "How could you get involved with a player you're supposed to cover? Isn't that a conflict of interest?"

Each conversation chipped away at his confidence, filling him with self-doubt. He'd entered this relationship to embrace love, not to become a scandal.

In the midst of it all, they found solace in their shared moments of vulnerability. They would sit on the balcony, sipping wine, allowing the city's nighttime energy to wash over them. In those moments, the world faded away, and it was just the two of them, navigating the complexities of love and life together.

As the fallout continued to unfold, Alex and Marcus learned the importance of leaning into each other's strength. They recognized that despite the turmoil, they had each other's backs. It wasn't just about surviving the storm; it was about emerging stronger on the other side, together.

The journey ahead was uncertain, but together they would confront the challenges, ready to fight for their love and reclaim their narratives amidst the chaos. They knew that in love, as in life, resilience was key. And they were ready to face whatever came next, hand in hand.

Just when it seemed that the storm could not get any darker, a glimmer of support emerged from an unexpected source—Marcus's teammates. Initially wary of the media frenzy, they began to rally around him, standing in solidarity against the tide of negativity.

It started with a casual tweet from Jordan, one of Marcus's closest friends on the team. "Proud to have Marcus Greene as my teammate. He's a warrior on and off the court. #LoveIsLove." The message resonated, gaining traction as fans started sharing their own messages of support, creating a wave of positivity amidst the backlash.

As the days passed, other teammates joined in, echoing similar sentiments. They wore shirts emblazoned with "Support Marcus" during warm-ups, making a statement that they stood by their teammate regardless of public opinion. News outlets picked up on the solidarity, and suddenly, the narrative began to shift.

The media was no longer just focused on the scandal; they were now highlighting the unity of the team. Stories emerged about how Marcus had always been there for his teammates, from late-night practices to supporting them through personal struggles. With each positive article, the tide began to turn.

"Look at this!" Marcus exclaimed one night, showing Alex his phone. "The support is overwhelming! People are standing up for me." There was a spark in his eyes that had been missing during the darker days.

Alex smiled, relief washing over him. "It's incredible. You deserve every bit of it. This is what true allies look like."

Amidst the shifting tides, Alex's editor, too, began to reconsider the story. Initially focused on distancing the paper from the controversy, she had seen the impact of the teammates' support and the public's response.

One afternoon, she called Alex back into her office, her demeanor noticeably softer. "I've been thinking," she started, avoiding eye contact for a moment before finally meeting his gaze. "Your piece on Marcus... I realize now it's not just about the scandal. There's a deeper narrative here—one of acceptance, bravery, and resilience. We can't ignore that."

Alex felt a swell of hope rise within him. "So, you're saying you want to run it?"

"I want to explore it," she clarified. "We need to present it in a way that highlights not just the relationship, but also the support he's receiving. It's a story about love in the face of adversity. I think it has the potential to resonate with a lot of people."

"Really?" Alex asked, almost incredulously. "After everything that's happened?"

"Yeah," she said, her voice firming. "The world needs more stories like this. We can still navigate the challenges, but we need to do it from a place of understanding rather than judgment."

As he left her office, Alex felt a renewed sense of purpose. He wanted to tell their story, not just as a scandal but as a testament to love conquering fear and adversity.

That evening, he met Marcus at a quiet café, the buzz of the world outside dimming to a soothing murmur. He could see the lingering tension in Marcus's eyes, but there was also a flicker of hope.

"I had a conversation with my editor today," Alex began, leaning in closer. "They want to pivot the story. It's going to focus on you, your teammates, and the love that's been pouring in from fans. It's not just about the scandal anymore—it's about your journey and the strength of your character."

Marcus's expression shifted from concern to surprise. "Really? You think they'll let us tell the whole story?"

"I believe they will. The narrative is changing, and we have the chance to shape it. This isn't just about us anymore; it's about everyone who feels like they have to hide. We can inspire people."

The corners of Marcus's mouth turned upward, a smile breaking through the weight of recent days. "I never thought I'd be standing in the spotlight like this—especially not for something so personal."

Alex reached across the table, taking Marcus's hand. "You're not just standing alone. You have your teammates, your fans, and me. We're all in this together."

With renewed determination, they spent the next few days crafting their story. They discussed everything—the challenges they had faced, the moments of doubt, and the overwhelming support that had begun to blossom around them.

The more they spoke, the more they realized that they had created a narrative not only about their love but also about community and acceptance. Each word was infused with their truth, a message that transcended the confines of a relationship and spoke to the heart of human experience.

As the article began to take shape, the atmosphere around them shifted. Friends, family, and fans rallied even more, sharing their own stories of love and acceptance in the face of adversity. Social media was ablaze with hashtags like #LoveWins and #SupportMarcus, transforming the conversation from one of scandal to one of celebration.

On the day the article was set to publish, Alex and Marcus felt a mix of excitement and trepidation. They sat together in Marcus's living room, each lost in their thoughts. "Whatever happens next, I'm ready," Marcus said quietly, squeezing Alex's hand.

"Me too," Alex replied, a smile spreading across his face. "No matter how this unfolds, we've already won by being true to ourselves."

And as the clock ticked down to the release, they both understood that this was just the beginning. They had faced the darkness and emerged stronger, bound together by love and the unwavering support of those around them. The fallout had transformed into a powerful story of resilience, and they were prepared to share it with the world, hand in hand.

As the days rolled on, the momentum of support continued to build, culminating in a highly anticipated public interview with Marcus. Scheduled just days after the backlash, the interview was designed to give him a platform to address the swirling rumors and reestablish his narrative.

Seated in a sleek studio adorned with sports memorabilia, Marcus appeared calm yet resolute. The interviewer, a seasoned sports journalist, began with safe questions about his performance and the upcoming season. But as the conversation progressed, it became clear that the topic of his personal life was inevitable.

"Marcus," the interviewer prompted, leaning in with curiosity, "there's been a lot of speculation about your relationship with Alex. How do you feel about the public's reaction?"

Marcus took a deep breath, his gaze steady as he considered his words. "You know, it's important to be honest with yourself and the people who support you," he began, a hint of a smile playing on his lips. "Alex has been an incredible part of my journey—not just as a journalist but as a person. He's challenged me, supported me, and shown me what it means to be true to myself."

The shift in the room was palpable. The interviewer's eyes widened, recognizing the depth of Marcus's words. "So you're saying you stand by him?"

"Absolutely," Marcus affirmed, his voice unwavering. "In times like these, it's crucial to have people who believe in you. Alex has stood by me through thick and thin, and I'm proud of the love we share, regardless of what anyone thinks."

As the interview aired live, fans and followers were captivated. Social media exploded with messages of support, many taking to platforms to express their admiration for Marcus's bravery. Hashtags like #SupportMarcus and #TeamAlex began trending, transforming what had felt like a scandal into a celebration of love and authenticity.

Alex watched the interview unfold from the comfort of his apartment, a mix of pride and disbelief washing over him. Marcus's words resonated with him, striking a chord deep within. "He really means it," Alex murmured to himself, his heart swelling with affection.

Messages flooded his phone almost immediately. Friends, acquaintances, and even strangers reached out, voicing their support. "I can't believe how brave Marcus is! Love is love!"

one message read. Another simply stated, "You both inspire me to be true to myself."

Each notification felt like a lifeline, reinforcing their resolve amidst the chaos. The sense of isolation that had shadowed them began to lift, replaced by a growing community of allies. They were no longer just fighting for their love in a vacuum; they were part of something larger, a movement that transcended their individual story.

After the interview aired, Alex and Marcus met at their usual spot, a cozy café tucked away from the hustle of the city. The atmosphere buzzed with energy, and as soon as Marcus walked in, the warmth of his presence filled the room.

"I just saw it," Alex said, his voice barely above a whisper. "What you said... it was beautiful."

Marcus smiled, the tension of the past few weeks easing off his shoulders. "I meant every word. I want people to know that love is worth fighting for, no matter the obstacles."

As they settled into their seats, the energy between them crackled with a mix of excitement and relief. They were still navigating the fallout, but for the first time, it felt like they were moving forward together.

"Did you see all the support online?" Marcus asked, pulling out his phone. He scrolled through the countless messages and reposts, his eyes lighting up with each new notification. "It's incredible how many people are rallying around us."

"I never expected this kind of response," Alex admitted, feeling a wave of gratitude. "It feels like we're not just surviving this—we're thriving."

With every passing hour, the messages of support continued to pour in, each one a reminder that they were not alone in their journey. They began planning ways to give back, brainstorming ideas for a charity initiative that focused on LGBTQ+ youth, ensuring that their story would inspire others.

As they shared laughter and dreams over coffee, a sense of purpose crystallized between them. They had faced the fallout, but rather than breaking them, it had forged a stronger bond. Their love story was no longer just about them; it had the potential to impact countless others.

Later that evening, as they walked back to Marcus's apartment, hand in hand, the night felt electric with possibility. The world around them had changed, and so had they. The journey ahead wouldn't be without its challenges, but armed with each other and the newfound support of their community, they were ready to face whatever came next.

Marcus paused under the soft glow of a streetlamp, turning to Alex. "We're in this together, right? No matter what?"

"Always," Alex replied, his heart full. "We've built something beautiful, and I wouldn't trade it for anything."

And with that, they moved forward, knowing that love, in its purest form, was the ultimate power they could wield against the world. The fallout had given them not just strength, but a renewed sense of purpose—a chance to make their love a beacon of hope for others navigating their own paths.

Chapter 10: Breaking Free

With the truth partially out, Marcus and Alex stepped into a new chapter of their relationship, one that was tinged with both excitement and trepidation. The weight of secrecy had lifted, replaced by a cautious sense of freedom. They had fought hard for their love, and now, as the world slowly began to accept them, they felt the exhilarating rush of possibilities unfold before them.

Their first outing as a publicly recognized couple took place at a local art exhibit, an event that Marcus had been eager to attend. "It's low-key enough that we can blend in," he had said, his eyes sparkling with anticipation. "Plus, I've always wanted to check out the new gallery downtown."

As they approached the venue, the familiar pulse of anxiety fluttered in Alex's stomach. Would fans recognize them? How would the media respond? But as Marcus linked his fingers with Alex's, the warmth of his grip instilled a sense of courage. This was their moment—one they had longed for, and they would embrace it together.

Inside the gallery, vibrant colors and intriguing sculptures surrounded them. The atmosphere buzzed with conversation, laughter, and the soft clinking of wine glasses. Marcus's presence drew the attention of a few fans, and Alex felt a rush of pride as they approached him for autographs and selfies. Marcus handled it all with grace, flashing his charming smile, while Alex stood by his side, beaming with a mix of admiration and affection.

"This feels amazing," Marcus said, leaning in to whisper in Alex's ear as they moved through the crowd. "It's like we're finally free to be ourselves."

Alex nodded, returning the warmth of Marcus's smile. "Just keep an eye out. We don't want to draw too much attention too soon."

They wandered through the gallery, pausing to admire the artwork, engaging in light conversation that felt effortless. It was a liberating experience—each laugh and shared glance deepening their connection. The tension that had accompanied their secret meetings dissipated, leaving room for a new kind of intimacy to flourish.

As the evening progressed, they gravitated toward a quieter corner of the gallery, away from the prying eyes of curious onlookers. "Can you believe how far we've come?" Alex asked, his voice barely above a whisper.

"I can," Marcus replied, his gaze serious yet soft. "But we have to stay smart. I don't want to jeopardize everything we've worked for."

"Agreed," Alex said, the reality of their situation grounding him. "But it's nice to enjoy this moment, even just for a little while."

Just then, a group of fans recognized Marcus and approached them. "Hey, Marcus! Can we get a picture with you?" one of them asked, excitement palpable in their voice.

"Of course!" Marcus replied, his smile widening. He positioned himself in front of the group, pulling Alex closer. The flash of cameras illuminated the moment, capturing not just the star athlete but also the man who stood proudly by his side.

As the fans walked away, giggling and buzzing with excitement, Alex felt a mix of joy and nervousness. "That was... surreal," he said, laughter bubbling up inside him.

"Yeah, but it feels good," Marcus said, squeezing Alex's hand. "We're no longer hiding. We're not just a rumor or a scandal. We're real."

After the exhibit, they decided to grab a late dinner at a nearby restaurant, choosing a cozy table in a dimly lit corner. The intimate atmosphere allowed them to relax and reflect on the night's events. They shared stories, laughter, and dreams, discussing everything from future plans to the art they had seen.

But as they enjoyed their meal, they couldn't escape the lingering caution that accompanied their new visibility. Each glance around the restaurant felt charged, as if someone might be watching. They were no longer just Alex and Marcus; they were a couple with a story that the world was eager to dissect.

"I hope people can see beyond the headlines," Alex said, concern etched on his face. "I don't want this to turn into just another scandal."

Marcus nodded thoughtfully. "It's going to take time. But we'll show them who we really are. Our relationship is about so much more than that. It's about love, respect, and support."

As they left the restaurant, a sense of exhilaration washed over them. The night air was crisp, and the streets felt alive with possibilities. Marcus pulled Alex closer, their shoulders brushing as they walked side by side.

"We're doing this," Marcus said, his voice low and filled with conviction. "Together."

"Together," Alex echoed, his heart swelling with hope. In that moment, he felt an unbreakable bond with Marcus, one that would carry them through whatever challenges lay ahead.

But just as they stepped onto the main street, a group of paparazzi emerged from the shadows, their cameras flashing like lightning. The bright lights momentarily blinded Alex, and his heart raced as he instinctively took a step closer to Marcus.

"Stay close," Marcus murmured, wrapping an arm around Alex's waist, grounding him amid the chaos.

As the questions and flashes intensified, Alex felt a mix of fear and defiance. This was their moment, their truth, and they would face it together.

"Marcus! Is it true that you're dating Alex?" one reporter shouted.

"Do you care to comment on the rumors?" another chimed in, snapping pictures relentlessly.

Marcus took a deep breath, turning to face the cameras with a confident smile. "Yes, it's true. Alex means a lot to me. I'm proud to be with him."

The statement hung in the air, and for a brief moment, the chaos faded away. Alex's heart raced with pride and fear, but most of all, with love. In that instant, he realized that this was their new reality—a life in the spotlight, but one they would navigate together, unafraid to show the world who they truly were.

As they walked away from the frenzy, hand in hand, Alex felt a surge of determination. They were breaking free from the chains of secrecy, stepping into the light as a couple ready to embrace whatever came next. Together, they would rewrite their narrative, forging a path defined by authenticity, love, and resilience.

The following weeks were a whirlwind of change for Alex and Marcus. The initial shock of their public declaration had faded, but the media storm continued to swirl around them. Determined to seize control of their narrative, Alex poured his energy into crafting an article that would tell their story on his terms.

Sitting at his desk late one evening, the glow of his laptop illuminating the room, Alex felt a mix of excitement and trepidation. He had witnessed firsthand the backlash against Marcus, the scrutiny they faced, and the cruel comments that accompanied their newfound visibility. But he also saw the support, the love, and the resilience that had emerged from the chaos. This was their chance to share not just the challenges but the beauty of their relationship.

With every keystroke, Alex aimed to encapsulate the truth of their journey. He wrote about the stolen moments, the laughter, and the vulnerability that had woven their lives together. He focused on the humanity behind the headlines, highlighting Marcus's character—not just as an NBA star but as a man unafraid to love deeply and openly.

The article took shape, weaving in quotes from their time together, anecdotes that painted a vivid picture of their connection. He recalled their first meeting, the spark of chemistry that had ignited their bond, and how they navigated the complexities of their hidden affair. He infused the piece with the raw emotions they had both experienced—fear, joy, anxiety, and ultimately, love.

As he neared the conclusion, Alex found the perfect way to encapsulate their story: "In a world eager to reduce love to a scandal, we are choosing to live boldly. Our relationship is not merely a chapter in the headlines; it's a testament to the power of love against all odds. We are more than what the world perceives—we are two individuals forging a path together, hand in hand, ready to face whatever challenges may come."

After a final review, he hit "send," transmitting the article to his editor with a sense of accomplishment that enveloped him. This was not just an article; it was a declaration of their love, an affirmation of their right to be together publicly.

The day of publication arrived, and Alex could barely contain his anticipation. He watched as the article went live, his heart pounding as he refreshed the page. The headline blared: "Beyond the Headlines: An Inside Look at Marcus Greene and Alex Bennett's Journey of Love." Beneath it, the text unfolded, revealing their story to the world.

Almost immediately, the responses began to flood in. Comments on social media ignited a wave of support, with readers praising Alex for his honesty and vulnerability. Many shared their own stories of love and acceptance, creating a ripple effect that resonated deeply across platforms.

"Thank you for sharing your truth!" one comment read. "This is the kind of love we need more of in the world." Another noted, "Finally, a beautiful story that isn't just about scandal. This is what love looks like!"

As the article gained traction, so did Marcus's public image. Fans began rallying around him, celebrating not just his basketball prowess but also his courage in embracing his personal life. The narrative shifted from scandal to acceptance, and it was clear that Alex's words were making an impact.

Marcus called Alex that evening, his voice brimming with excitement. "I just read the article. It's incredible, Alex! You captured everything perfectly."

"Thanks, Marcus. I wanted the world to see you for who you really are," Alex replied, a smile spreading across his face. "Not just the basketball player, but the man who has shown me so much love."

"I can't believe how much support we're getting," Marcus said, his tone a mix of disbelief and joy. "It feels like we're finally being seen, not as a scandal but as a couple."

As they spoke, Alex felt the weight of their journey lift, replaced by a sense of hope and possibility. They had taken a leap of faith, and it was paying off. The darkness that had clouded their relationship began to recede, giving way to a brighter, more promising future.

Over the next few days, the positive response continued to grow. Their story was shared widely, sparking discussions about love, acceptance, and the importance of authenticity. Alex found himself inundated with messages from fellow journalists, eager to feature Marcus in a more profound light—far from the sensationalism that had once surrounded him.

"We're doing this, Marcus," Alex said during one of their late-night calls, the excitement palpable in his voice. "We're changing the narrative."

"Together," Marcus affirmed, a sense of conviction in his tone. "And we'll keep doing it. This is just the beginning."

The renewed focus on Marcus's career also brought unexpected opportunities. Endorsements began rolling in, not only for his performance on the court but for his newfound role as a symbol of love and authenticity. Brands sought to align themselves with him, recognizing that his story resonated with fans who valued integrity and courage.

As the dust began to settle, Alex and Marcus found themselves in a more stable place, able to enjoy their relationship openly while still being mindful of the complexities that came with fame. They embraced their newfound freedom, taking walks in the park, dining at their favorite restaurants, and attending events without the shadow of secrecy hanging over them.

One evening, as they strolled hand in hand along a moonlit path, Marcus paused to pull Alex close. "I've never felt this alive," he said, his voice barely above a whisper. "I'm so grateful for you and everything we've accomplished together."

Alex smiled, feeling a rush of emotion. "We've fought hard for this. It's ours to cherish."

Underneath the stars, they shared a kiss, a moment that solidified their commitment to each other. They had broken free from the constraints of their past, stepping into a future filled with promise, authenticity, and above all, love.

As the days turned into weeks, Alex and Marcus found their rhythm in this new chapter of their lives. With the burden of secrecy lifted, they embraced their relationship fully, cherishing every moment together. Late-night conversations morphed into plans for the future, each discussion infused with excitement and determination.

One evening, nestled on the couch in Alex's apartment, they flipped through photos on Marcus's phone—snapshots of their outings, candid moments stolen in the midst of their whirlwind romance. Alex laughed at a picture of Marcus mid-laugh, his eyes crinkling in delight. "You look like a kid in a candy store," he teased.

"Can you blame me?" Marcus grinned, his expression brightening. "I've got everything I ever wanted right here." He turned to Alex, the sincerity in his eyes cutting through the lighthearted atmosphere. "I want us to keep building on this. I want a life with you."

Alex felt a warmth bloom in his chest. "I want that too, more than anything." He paused, considering the challenges they had already faced. "But we know it won't be easy. There will always be people who want to tear us down."

Marcus nodded, his expression serious but resolute. "I'm ready for that. We've faced so much together already. I know we can handle anything that comes our way." He reached for Alex's hand, intertwining their fingers. "We'll support each other, no matter what."

The two began discussing their dreams—a cozy home filled with laughter, maybe a dog to complete their family. They talked about traveling, experiencing new cultures together, and attending games in different cities, hand in hand, their love on full display. Alex envisioned writing a book about their journey, showcasing not just the ups and downs but the beauty of their relationship and the lessons learned along the way.

"Imagine a world where we can inspire others to be true to themselves," Alex mused, excitement tingling in his veins. "I want to share our story, not just for us but for anyone who feels they have to hide who they are."

Marcus's eyes sparkled with enthusiasm. "I love that idea! We can show them that love conquers all, that being authentic is worth every struggle." He leaned closer, their foreheads touching, the intimacy of the moment grounding them in their shared vision.

As they planned their future, the reality of their circumstances lingered in the background. Marcus was still an NBA star, and Alex was still a journalist. The public eye would always be there, but they had each other—a bond forged in secrecy and tested through adversity. They knew they had to navigate the challenges that lay ahead with grace and strength.

One afternoon, they decided to take a stroll in the park, hand in hand, where they could blend in with the throng of everyday life. The sun dipped low in the sky, casting a golden hue over everything, and for a brief moment, the world felt perfect. They paused by a fountain, the sound of water creating a peaceful backdrop as they shared their dreams and aspirations.

"I want us to be open about our relationship," Marcus declared, his voice firm yet tender. "I don't want to hide anymore. I want to be proud of who we are together."

Alex smiled, warmth spreading through him. "I agree. We'll do it on our own terms, though. No rushing, just us taking the steps that feel right."

With a renewed sense of purpose, they walked back to the apartment, their hearts aligned in a shared vision. They might face scrutiny and judgment, but they were committed to weathering whatever storms came their way. The challenges were a part of their journey, not the end of it.

As they entered the apartment, Marcus pulled Alex close, the familiar spark igniting between them. "No matter what happens, we'll face it together," he promised, his voice low and sincere.

"Together," Alex echoed, feeling the truth of those words resonate deep within him. In that moment, they both knew that love, when nurtured and fought for, could create a life filled with hope, laughter, and endless possibilities.

They leaned in, sharing a kiss that felt like a promise—one of resilience, courage, and a bright future. With their hearts intertwined, they were ready to embrace the journey ahead, hand in hand, side by side, knowing that love was their ultimate strength.

Also by Dow Jones

Breaking the Rules
Courtside Secrets
Love's Dividends